LOCKWOOD LIONS

✓ P9-BYG-742

The Lockwood High cheer squad has it *all*—sass, looks, and all the right moves. But everything isn't always as perfect as it seems. Because where there's cheer, there's drama. And then there's the ballers—hot, tough, and on point. But what's going to win out—life's pressures or their NFL dreams?

BLAKE BALLER *Swag*

Cocky quarterback Blake Strong's
number one goal is to stay in the game.
*Will he realize there is more to life
than football?*

ALL THAT

Stephanie Perry Moore
& Derrick Moore

SADDLEBACK
EDUCATIONAL PUBLISHING

BALLER SWAG

All That

No Hating

Do You

Be Real

Got Pride

SADDLEBACK
EDUCATIONAL PUBLISHING
www.sdlback.com

ISBN-13: 978-1-61651-884-4
ISBN-10: 1-61651-884-7
eBook: 978-1-61247-618-6

Printed in Guangzhou, China
0212/CA21200344

16 15 14 13 12   1 2 3 4 5

To Dr. Franklin and Shirley Perry Sr.
(Stephanie's Parents)

*We can be all that because you two have always
been in our corner. We want you to know that
your love for us and our children helps us soar.
Thank you for being great examples, and
thank you for showing us the way. We hope every
reader learns they too can be dynamic.*

*You are the best parents
anyone could ask for ... we love you!*

ACKNOWLEDGEMENTS

When you are a competitor, wanting to win is natural. You prepare for your opponent. You train extra hard. You listen to your coach. When you are good, you want your teammates to be just as stellar. You push them. You encourage them. And you do not let them settle for less. However, as focused as you are, sometimes life happens and throws off your focus. It may be grades, an illness, money problems, girl drama, or anything that gets you down. We know it is hard to have swag when you feel sad.

Nevertheless, we want you to stay focused on your goals while you are going through it. Be a leader in the midst of the strife. Your demeanor can uplift those around you and can change the outcome for the better. The message we want you to grasp … being a true baller does not just mean strutting your stuff when life is good. It means being the man and holding your head up high when you go through tough times.

Acknowledgements

Here is huge thanks to all those who help us stay driven and prolific.

To Derrick's mother, Ann Redding, your love is all that.

To our publisher, especially Tim McHugh, your idea for this series was all that.

To our extended family: brothers, Dennis Perry and Victor Moore, sister, Sherry Moore, godparents, Walter and Marjorie Kimbrough, nephews, Franklin Perry III and Kadarius Moore, and godsons, Danton Lynn, Dakari Jones, and Dorian Lee, your place in our life is all that to us.

To our assistants: Alyxandra Pinkston and Joy Spencer, your work ethic is all that.

To our friends who mean so much: Jim and Deen Sanders, Antonio and Gloria London, Chett and Lakeba Williams, Bobby and Sarah Lundy, Harry and Torian Colon, Byron and Kim Forest, Donald and Deborah Bradley, your friendship is all that.

To our teens: Dustyn, Sydni, and Sheldyn, the meaning and purpose you give to our lives is all that.

To the media specialists and educational companies across the country who support us: especially, Rhonda Sapp from Delaney Educational, your unending support is all that.

To our new readers, whom we know can apply themselves and be vigorous readers, your efforts to become
better is all that.

And to our Lord, who has given us each other and our
dreams. Your love for us is all that.

CHAPTER 1

High Expectations

Son, why are you out here on my practice field if you're not going to really work? Blake Strong, live up to your name. Out here looking weak, giving half effort, and leading like a sissy," my dad said all up in my grill.

It was the beginning of July, the first practice of the summer. Football was all that I had been training for. It was my junior year—supposedly my time to step up and show college scouts I could play. However, with my dad, Coach Bradley Strong, former NFL player with the Tampa Bay Buccaneers, pushing me so hard, I wanted to quit.

"Did you drink the gallon of water last night so you won't cramp up? You know you can't come

1

out in this heat and not be pre-hydrated. Did you drink the shake this morning? If I don't stay on you, like people have to do with pee-wee players, who knows what you'll end up being. I expect you to come out here and give me one hundred ten percent. It's like you're giving me fifty percent effort. Absolutely unacceptable ... go run."

That was all I wanted him to say. I wanted to be dismissed so I could get away from him. I did love my dad, but he was overboard. Not only was he a fanatic football father, but he also was an obsessed coach. Put those two together, and one could see my world was miserable.

"Defense, huddle up," he said when I made it to the track.

Going into the season, our team was ranked one of the top in our region in the state. We were stacked with talent on both sides of the ball. All of our talent was coming back. Most of us were juniors. We had one of the best wide receivers in the country, Landon King, the best middle linebacker, my cousin Brenton Strong, and the most ferocious defensive end, Leo Steele. I was one of the top quarterbacks. With great players on both sides of the ball, my dad could smell a state title, and he was pushing super hard.

Landon was my boy, and he ran up beside me. "Don't let him get to you like that."

Venting, I said, "You don't understand. He's getting on my nerves. He pushes, and I push back, giving him all I got. Then he pushes harder, like he wants me to break. Nothing I do is good enough. Having a dad like him is excruciating."

Making jokes, Landon said, "Uh-oh, look at you, partna, using big words *excursiate ... excr ...* What?"

"Don't play, and don't try to make me laugh," I said, smiling anyway. "You know I've been studying for the SAT. I better be, too, because you just can't have skills on the field and not be able to do well on those tests. You feelin' me, son?"

Landon picked up the pace, as I did, and said, "I know. I know. You said it to me tons and tons of times. The lower GPA I have, the higher SAT score I'm required to have."

Being real, I breathed, "Exactly, but it's all good because you're pulling a three-point-o. But opening up those books and learning those large words would not hurt."

Landon stopped running. "Well, I see my job's done here," he said, not wanting me to get on him.

I jogged back over to him and said, "What do you mean?"

"You can't be upset at your dad anymore. You're back in rare Blake form."

"What does that mean?" I questioned, frustrated with Landon's attempts to cheer me up.

"You know ... pushing people and tryna get the best outta your team. Don't stop. You're really a clone of your dad," Landon said, being my best buddy.

I was tired, exhausted, and beat, but I looked over at the football field and saw the almost hundred athletes and pondered on my duty. I realized that though I had the reputation for being all that, I worked for it. I needed to keep on working for it because I was playing for them. Though I wanted to grab my dad by the collar and absolutely go off on him for being a jerk, I figured I would show him I had what it took.

When the time came for drills, as the quarterback of the team, I had everybody hustling. My energy was high, and the team was feeding off that as if I were fuel for our engine. Personally, I was doing my thing as well. For ten balls straight, my passes were executed and caught right on point. I had the short passes down, the long bombs tight, and all the middle deep throws were accurate too.

After practice my dad called me to his office. "Sorry, I got on you pretty hard out there earlier today, but what I just saw, that's what's gonna get you a D1 scholarship. You wanna be a Florida Gator? Keep ballin' like that and you'll be wearing the blue and orange, baby."

I did not want to fuss with my father, but he knew I wanted to go to Notre Dame. Yeah, it was not in the powerhouse Southeastern Conference. It was not close to home, but it was my dream school.

Truthfully, I did not want to live in his shadow. He'd wanted me to be a wide receiver. He said African American quarterbacks had it harder and did not really have a chance in the NFL. However, when I told him I wanted to play that position, and he saw that I was smart, determined, and talented, he helped me learn the game. Now that it was almost time for Friday night lights, I was ready.

Pushing more, he asked, "So what time you going to the gym?"

"I just thought I'd chill out for a minute, Dad. I went to the gym yesterday and the day before that. I was watching film last night. I just wanted to hang out and take Charli to the mall. She wants to pick up something for her mom's birthday," I uttered, knowing that probably wasn't the truth, but wanting to explain every detail so he would cut me slack.

Getting no slack cut, he voiced, "Take her out to the mall? You aren't no chauffeur, and this isn't the weekend."

Completely frustrated, I said, "Dang, Dad. It's the summer. Everything you've asked me to do, I've done. Why you on me so much? Ease up some."

"Oh? You think I'm on you?" my dad said, as he stood behind his desk just inches away from me. "Dang, boy, you make me so angry."

I got spankings until I was almost in high school. These days I could sometimes see in my dad's eyes that he wanted to take off his belt and use it. However, I was coming into my own.

Being clear, I was not the baddest thing at Lockwood High School because I was his son. I had earned my stripes. I was not arrogant, but I was confident. Fellas admired me, and ladies wanted to get with this. However, I had a girl who was model material. Charli Black was da bomb, and I was super ready to really set off fireworks with her.

I moved to Georgia when my parents' jobs got relocated here in the ninth grade. So much changed that year. The biggest changes were that the whippings stopped and my strength grew. He could not come at me any way he wanted and think I was going to take it. I had respect for him, but he was close to losing it. He was almost schizo-phrenic. His ways mirrored the disease. One day he was sweet; the next day he was a maniac.

Our relationship was hanging on by a thread, and he definitely didn't strengthen it when he said, "Why don't you act like Brenton?

He's never a smart aleck. He always works harder than I ask, and he wants my help."

I just looked at my dad. I was not about to answer his idiotic question, and I certainly was not going to feel bad that I did not try to compare myself or be like my precious cousin. Brenton is his sister's son. We were born a week apart. He was the oldest, and he would not let me forget. I truly believed if my dad could have his way, he would have switched us at birth.

Like stabbing my heart with a knife and twisting it, my dad said, "Brenton's over there struggling with my sister. The boy don't have nothing. Here you got everything you want, and you just take it for granted, son."

Dad took pity on his nephew. It was not my fault Brenton's dad got my aunt knocked up, and he had not been seen or heard from since. It *is* my problem that my dad tries to overcompensate. He tries to not only be my cousin's uncle, but his absent father as well. When my dad took me to the zoo, he had to take Brenton too. When my dad bought me a pair of shoes, he had to buy Brenton a pair as well. We were not twins. We were not even brothers, and it truly got under my skin that he thought Brenton was superior to me. Yeah, I knew my dad loved Brenton's toughness. My dad was a linebacker, but I wanted the prima donna spot. So what that I didn't like getting hit? Last time I checked, no team can win without the quarterback.

"Make sure you take Brenton home first, and don't be out long with *that* girl," my dad said, realizing that I deserved a break. "But just so you know, I will have my foot on your throat till the day you leave here. So accept it."

I could only nod. He flung his hand in the air, dismissing me. At that moment I wished for the day I was outta there. It could not come soon enough.

As I stepped out of my dad's office, my cousin was in my face.

It wasn't Brenton's fault that my dad wanted him as a son instead of me. But I wanted to knock his pearly whites out of his mouth when he said, "Ready?"

In all honesty, Brenton had not done anything to me but have my back, so with no beef I said, "Yeah, man. Let's roll."

I looked back in my dad's office, and I could only hope that I would make him proud. I was trying. Eventually he was going to see it because I set the bar even higher for myself than he did. Booyah.

"Hey, baby, can't wait to see ya. What time should I be ready?" my girlfriend, Charli, said.

Just hearing her voice got me all excited. I so wanted to be with her. Her image would not leave my mind. I would be lifting weights, and I would imagine her standing in front of me. I would be asleep, and I would think of her lying next to me. Sometimes I would be driving, and I would imagine her sitting straight on top of me. It was our time.

However, my girl was a little too good, and though she knew I was not a bad boy, she thought I was pretty good too. I had yet to fully experience all of my manhood. However, this was my junior year, my time to come into my own in a lot of ways. Honestly, I only thought it was fair that we'd take our relationship to the next level. I'd done things her way for two years, but now it was time for her to show me and not just tell me how much she truly cared.

"You can't wait to see me, huh?" I said, licking my lips. I could practically taste her neck that I desperately wanted to suck.

"You know I can't," her sultry voice responded.

"We'll see," I voiced strongly, unsure if we were on the same page.

"Blake, what are you inferring?"

Blunt as I could be, I shouted, "Inferring, referring, blatantly saying, I'm telling you ... I miss you. I had a hard practice, and I need some love."

"I gotcha," she said without hesitating.

"Fo' real? You know what I'm talking about, and you got me? You and me? Today? Us?" I said skeptically. I needed her to fully understand what I meant.

"Babe, just come get me. I'm wearing something extra special for you," Charli Black teased.

"I'm on my way," I said, as I spun off in the parking lot.

"Why you pressuring that girl?" Brenton said before I could even say bye to my girl.

"Why you all in my conversation?" I said to my cousin, wishing he would hush up and quit being the purity police.

But I don't even know why I asked him that question. I knew he liked my girl. They went way back to middle school, elementary school, or something. Before I moved here, they used to be tight, but he wasn't making a move. I remember living in South Carolina, and all he kept talking about was this cute girl who all the fellas were bending over tryna rap to her. To him she was an angel. The way she walked, the way she talked, and the way she looked, had him smitten.

I remembered going to school with him the first day of ninth grade. I saw this girl whose name I did not know. She was stunning, and I did a double-take. I followed her around, and I was so happy that we were in the same class. When I found out that she was the girl he'd been going on and on about, I was already hooked. What Brenton didn't like was that she was hooked on me too. Practically all ninth grade he and I did not talk. We played ninth grade ball together, and in practice he tried to kill me.

It was not until my dad talked to him that there were no more hits on the quarterback in practice. At first my dad thought it was good that I got punched around, but Brenton wasn't letting up. That whole year more girls were coming at me, but I stayed true to Charli. After Brenton saw I was loyal, I won his trust back. We were blood, and I did not go after his girl intentionally. Once he understood that, he truly could not blame me for liking her the way I did.

Last year got a little rocky. Only holding hands with Charli didn't sit right with me. But if I even thought about getting out of line by trying to talk to someone else, my cousin appeared out of nowhere and was there as my conscience to keep me straight and true with Charli.

"It ain't going down like that this year, cuz," I said to Brenton, as we rode in the car.

"What are you talking about?" he asked with attitude.

"You watching me twenty-four-seven," I uttered boldly, as he knew doggone well what I was talking about. "You don't even want me to have friends who are girls. I got this with Charli. Go get some business of your own, man. Dang. She got four friends and ain't none of them with nobody. I could see you not wanting to be with big-mouth Eva, but her twin sister, Ella, is fine. She's sweet, and she won't say two words back

at you. And Randal with that mixed latte skin …
She's so shy, and so are you. Yeah, Randal might
be right up your alley."

"Who says I'm shy?" Brenton denied.

Peeved, irritated, and annoyed, I forcefully
said, "I'm just saying, get some business."

"Please, cuz, I warned you enough. Make
sure you handle yours before you don't have
none in that area," my cousin bluntly said to me.

What was he trying to say? Was he going to
take my girl or something? She was where she
wanted to be. She loved me too much to even
think about him. I was not worried, and I was
not thinking about him. I gave him a look that
spoke just that. Before the two of us tore each
other's heads off in my car, I was interrupted by
a ring of the cell phone. I looked down, and it was
a number I did not recognize. Brenton looked at
my phone and saw it wasn't Charli.

Keeping my hands on the wheel and ignoring
his uptight gesture, I answered the call. "Hello?"

I hate to drive like a nerd, but Brenton man-
aged to tell my dad everything. When around
him, I had to act like a Boy Scout. Last thing I
needed was my father revoking my keys.

A shaky voice coughed and said, "Hey, Blake. This is Trina from Dekalb County. We met at the skating rink a couple of weeks ago. You said you were gonna call me, but since you haven't, I figured I would call you."

I squinted because I could not remember who the girl was. I hung out at a lot of places: the skating rink, the bowling alley, and the mall. Lately, I had been at the gym and on the field. When I was out, I had taken girls' numbers because they handed them to me, but I didn't give mine to mere strangers.

"How'd you get my number?" I asked.

"I know someone who knows someone who gave it to me. That's not a problem, is it?"

Hesitating, I finally said, "Nah. So what's up? Um … what can I do for you?"

Truly forward, the Trina girl offered me a present. "Well, I was wondering if you wanted to see me. Today's my birthday, and I was wondering if you wanted to see me in my birthday suit."

I laughed. It was a gift I didn't want. I laughed again.

"Nah, I'm straight," I finally responded, finishing up the call.

I did not even know who Trina was, or why she was throwing herself at me. Why do girls do that? That's probably why I liked Charli so much. We had something strong, and she was still trying to hold out on me. As badly as I wanted to *really* become a man, it was not going to be with some Trina, Trick, or Cherry.

As soon as I hung up with her, the phone rang again. It was a girl named Jackie, and Jackie had my attention. I knew who she was. She had curves that she didn't mind showing in her low-cut blouses and short skirts. None of my boys had bragging rights on getting with that yet, and she had become locker-room talk. She was the hot topic of conversation because everyone wanted to know if she tasted as good as she looked. The only problem for me was I was already taken. However, the connection I felt to her showed in my voice.

Happy to see her name pop up on the ID, I said, "Hey, Jackie!"

"You didn't call me back last night," she said, making me feel guilty.

"Well, I can't talk right now, and it's like I told you last night. We can be friends, but I got a girl."

"It's cool. I'm not giving up on you, you know. We'll be together soon. When I put my mind to something happening, I don't let up until it's done," she said.

"I believe that. I'll speak to you later, okay?"

"Count on it," she said, obviously wanting me.

When I got to my aunt's house, my cousin didn't want to get out. "You playing with fire, boy."

Ticked, I said, "And what you gonna do, run back and tell on me?"

"Just when I think you are going to do right, you ..." Brenton said. He paused and got out. "You do dumb stuff. I'm not gonna baby-sit you, police you, or monitor your every move. Just know you've been warned. You not gonna hurt my girl."

He slammed the door. He was angry, but was he right? The last person I wanted to hurt was Charli. She was gonna have to step up. I had needs, and she needed to meet them or else.

I always considered myself a gentleman and certainly didn't mean to storm away from Charli in the middle of the food court, but she wasn't saying what I wanted to hear. She talked a good game before we met up, but as soon as I became transparent and told her that I needed more, she shut me down.

Of course the first person I'd run into was Wax. Yeah, that was his nickname. Waxton was his last name, but I don't remember what his first name was because we all just called him Wax. He loved the nickname. He bragged that he squeezed between linemen because he was as slippery as wax. He was a senior and the starting running back for our team. Wax was the world's biggest player, but not as good at toting the mail like he claimed, getting a few too many fumbles last year. He had two girls following right behind him. His dad owned the largest nightclub in town, and I heard some of what happened behind those walls. I was just a little sick of Wax ragging me.

"Hey, Strong, you need come over here and get you a little bite. You too pent up. I seen my man kicking chairs and stuff. What? Yo' girl holding out still?" Wax teased.

"Man, gone," I said, as I walked round him.

I had already eaten, but I did mean to purpose my steps to Dairy Queen. It was not the treat I wanted, but under the circumstances, it was going to have to suffice. Wax turned around and said something to the girls. They stepped aside, and he motioned for me to come and follow him around the corner.

"Look, I'm tryna go to the dome this year. I got all these offers coming my way, and I'm just tryna decide where I'ma sign come February. In order for me to stay cream of the crop, my quarterback has got to be on point. If our passing game is tight, I can fool the defense and steal twenty yards. I need you happy, not frustrated," Wax said with a wink.

That was the first time Wax gave anyone besides himself any type of thought. Since I lived with Wax's coach, I knew he was puffing about all of the college letters coming to his mailbox. However, I did believe Wax was gonna give the season his all, and I knew I needed to be on top of my game so Wax could shine. What did he want to give me to make sure I relaxed? I was not taking any roofies or anything, so what was his angle?

Talking to him straight, I said, "Man, I know you smoke that stuff, but that's not me."

"Whatever, I'm not tryna get you to take a puff. Though one day in your perfect life, taking a hit would be cool. What I know you do is make yourself feel good," he said, as he balled his fist and made hand motions up and down.

I frowned at his insult. Shoot, even if that was my pastime, it was my business. Wax trying to pressure me was getting under my skin like a nasty fungus.

"I'm just keeping it real. It's time to let a little lady do what she was put on this earth to do. I know you got a girl. Ditch her, and you can keep your business on the low, low. I got two chicks. So go on and drop your honey off, meet me at an apartment my dad gave me the keys to, and you can have a good time."

He motioned for the girls to come to us, and as they walked, their miniskirts flared up. They both stood really close to me, and the exotic dance moves they were doing to each other made me almost lose my mind.

However, like I have to do when I'm tired of working out, I mustered up the strength to look past them. I saw Charli on the phone. Her mannerisms suggested that she was upset, but how could I be there for her when I felt that she wasn't there for me? Jones in my pants had a mind of its own, and as it started to rise, I realized I did need that ice cream to cool off.

Without needing his approval, I stepped away and said, "I'm straight, Wax."

"Another time then," Wax said, as the girls placed their hands all over him.

Thankfully, before I got caught, I was where I was supposed to be. Actually, ordering a Blizzard was on point because I needed some snow to rain on me to get my mind off of where it was.

I thought Wax didn't get the message when I felt a female hand on my back. However, before I could fuss, my frown turned into a smile when I saw Jackie. She was looking sexier than the girls with Wax and definitely more my speed. She wasn't trashy, just appealing.

"I didn't know you were coming here," she said, stepping closer. "I hate that because I'm with my girls. Oh, but I'm not driving. You wanna give me a ride home? No one's there. We can talk." Jackie laughed.

Looking behind her, I still saw Charli on the phone. I figured she was talking about me to her girls. I had a woman who didn't care to please me, but what stood in front of me certainly did want to make me happy. Jackie saw I was distracted and looked back.

"Oh, you can't take me home; you're here with her."

"You know I have a girlfriend, so you gotta stop coming at me hard like this," I backed away.

"Here's your Blizzard, sir," the restaurant employee said.

"You want something?" I mistakenly asked Jackie.

"So you care," she said, looking me up and down.

Knowing my girl was waiting for me to get back to the table, I said, "No, I'm just being a gentleman. Would you like something?"

"I don't want any ice cream, but I do want something," Jackie said, peering through my soul.

She moved a little closer, and I was already excited. The connection was obviously not as strong as the one with Charli, but something was there, and it was more than I thought I'd ever feel for someone else.

"Imagine the possibilities," she said, biting her lip and shaking her hips.

"You talking a good game. Why do you like me?" I asked, wondering why this Jackie girl appealed to me besides the obvious.

"Forget you being cool, fine, and smart. You've got heart. I've watched you over the last couple of years. You are amazing. Your loyalty to Charli is impressive. But why her? She is just a girl who is cute but also an annoying gnat. I'm sure she has her purpose, but who knows what it is."

Not the answer I was looking for, I said, "You talking about surface stuff."

"Okay, let me be real. When I said heart, I've seen you take up for the underdog," she said, piquing my interest. "Yeah, you know ... the boys who get bullied at our school ... nobody messes with them when you're around. The girls who don't look too pretty ... you speak to them. You don't know how much it makes their day to have the hottest boy around be nice to them. It means a lot. You are not like these other boys here, going through the motions. You've got drive, and I want you to ride me."

I was sipping on my straw. I almost choked on the cold contents sliding down my throat. Jackie had a part of me that Charli might not ever be able to pull back.

Making my chest rise with her touch, Jackie said, "You're maturing, and the little girl you're going with isn't growing up as fast as you. Why should you settle for an okay relationship when you can have something way better? I know you, Blake. You like me, and its okay because you should have high expectations."

CHAPTER 2

Guard Up

Oh, so you're just going to have an attitude with me the whole ride home?" I said to Charli, as she sat on the passenger seat of my car with her arms folded.

"Please, Blake, give me some credit. Like I'm supposed to be all cool with the fact that I caught my guy showing his full grill up in some girl's face. You were so into her you didn't even see me walking up to you."

"But I introduced you guys," I said, trying to show her that I was not keeping anything a secret.

"And how'd that work out for ya?" Charli asked, as she looked out of the window to get even more distance between us.

Needing my girl to ease up, I said, "Just talk to me. Don't sit in here and put a wall up. You know I hate that, Charli."

"What do you want, Blake? For me to fall all over you like every other girl in our school? I didn't think I had to show you how much I cared. I thought you knew it. The nerve of that girl flirting with you right in front of me, saying she had enough girlfriends ... insinuating that she was looking for a boyfriend. So wassup, Blake? You tell me? You say don't be upset because it's no big deal, but you have feelings for this girl, don't you? You were chasing too hard."

"No," I said quickly, knowing a part of me was lying.

Trying to calm her down, I said, "We have made it a long time, Charli. So many people try to break us up; said we couldn't make it. Girls are after me. Guys are after you. Some guys are after me, and some girls are after you." She did not laugh at that moment. "Come on, baby, lighten up."

"Why you got jokes? You know there's some of everything at this school now, right or wrong."

"Tons of people been trying to split us apart. That's all I'm saying."

It was not right to give her an ultimatum and tell her to give it up to me or she was going to lose me. I was not that kind of guy, and I certainly did not want to hurt her like that. However, as we drove past a few hotels, I wanted to turn in there so bad, get a room, and go to work. I knew I cared for her more than any girl out there, and I had no doubt if my needs were met, she would not have to catch me flirting with another.

On the flip, what was *I* going to do when I knew that was not what she wanted. Since I was confused, I said the only thing I knew at the time. I went into Blake mode.

Stroking her hair, I said, "You know I care about you, girl."

Which was true because I did. And until I decided what I was going to do, there was no need to get her even more upset. I did want to feel her lips on mine, and if I did not do something quickly that was never going to happen. Before I dropped her off, I pulled up to a fast food restaurant, parked in the back, leaned over to her, took her hand, and kissed it. I stroked her hair again, tickled her a bit, and before she knew what was happening, our lips were locked, and her guard was down.

"I just don't want to lose you," she said, as she was feeling me too.

"You keep making me feel like this, baby, and you won't," I said, as I kissed her again. "It's hard, but I can wait."

"Oh, Blake," she said, melting like butter on a hot roll in my arms. "Soon, baby, soon."

I learned early how to stroke folks. You know, telling them what they want to hear. Now that Charli was satisfied, I knew she and I were good. She better make good soon because my patience was wearing thin.

When I dropped her off, I turned my phone back on. I had to play it that way because I couldn't give Charli any reason to question me about my phone calls, which ended up being a smart thing because I had six messages: five from girls, and one from my boy, Landon.

"Wassup, dude?" I said when I called him back.

"Trying to reach out to you. I'm over Mick's house, and there is a hottie sweating me to get you over here."

"Who, man? You know I'm out with Charli."

"Boy, don't play me," Landon said, really knowing me well.

"If your phone is on, you ain't with no Charli."

Landon seemed to know everyone in the county and had friends across town. In my opinion, they were trouble. Mick and his boys were part of a gang. I didn't want anybody getting the wrong idea, thinking that because I was hanging out, I was interested. The Axes were known as some of the hardest brothers in the ATL. They were into robbing, raping, and killing. They just weren't playing big and bad, they were brutal.

"Nah, dawg, I'm straight," I said to Landon, hating that my friend wanted to fit in so bad.

He was from a fine, upstanding family. His dad was pastor of a mega-church, and I believe because his father gave so much time taking care of his congregation, Landon resented it and was over-compensating by trying to lose his good-boy image by hanging with thugs.

"All right, if you don't want to come here, we can meet up some place else. The Jackie girl on the dance team won't let up about you, partna."

I knew if I got with Jackie again today, I would not be able to control my loins. But the thought of seeing her thighs once more made me cave like an avalanche. "Seeing her would be cool."

Sensing my hesitancy, Landon said, "How about I meet you up at the bowling alley? We can play Jackie and her girl in a couple of games. No biggie."

"I don't know, man," I said, thinking about what all that could possibly lead to.

Just like going to Mick's house could appear I was interested in the gang, if I went to the bowling alley, Jackie would think I was interested in her. That might be just as deadly. My mom taught me about women. Her theory was that if they were showing the world all they had, then they were probably giving it away too easy and could be carrying a venereal disease. While something about Jackie was intriguing, it might not be worth it.

Pleading, Landon said, "Come on, man. Help a brother out. I'm trying to get with KaydaKay."

"Who?" I asked, as that name made me think she needed to be left wherever she was.

"It's Jackie's girl. She straight. Ain't nothing wrong with bowling. Thought you were your own man. Didn't know Charli had you tied down. Start barking, dude."

I guess I wasn't the only one who knew how to say the right words to get the right reaction out of people. I did not like being called a punk, and I certainly was not a puppet or Charli's dog.

Hastily, I agreed. Before I even had time to let my conscience take over, I pulled up at the Lanes. I didn't know what Landon thought was appropriate lady-on-the-arm material, but Kay-daKay looked exactly how I had imagined her. Tore up from the floor up. I had seen all kinds of hairstyles in the ATL, but I had never seen white, pink, and green braids. That was for good reason. I didn't need to. She had to be a size 20 wearing a size 2. For real, she looked a hot mess, and if the optometrist was open, I would have dragged Landon there to see if he needed glasses.

Landon came up behind me and said, "Dang, man. You got to stare at her like that ... your boojie behind."

Whispering, I said, "Whatever, dude. She look like if you lay down with her, you going to rise up with something a dawg don't want."

When Jackie came over to me she said, "Is something wrong?"

I said, "Is that your girlfriend?"

"No, she's my cousin, and preacher boy is intrigued. Why you judging her though? I see your nose up in the air, like she's not your speed. You think you too good for folks?"

I actually had to ponder that question. My dad called it the eyeball test. People see you and immediately put you into some type of category. If you don't want negative thoughts, then make yourself look presentable. When I looked at this KaydaKay girl, she screamed nothing but ghetto fab. If this was Jackie's cousin, what kind of family did Jackie come from? As a dude trying to get with her, I might think it's enticing for Jackie to wear low-cut stuff, but if she was my girl, the dress standards would have to change. Jackie seemed too strong-willed to change. Therefore, the possibility that we could have something was dissipating.

"You think you're better than me," she said, as she saw I was unimpressed with her cousin and her tone.

I like that she said what was on her mind. I merely had a problem that she was naïve with the way the world viewed people. If you want to be taken seriously, dress the part.

Explaining, I said, "I just don't understand why you got to flaunt everything you got all the time. It makes me think—"

"What? That I'm fast," she said, cutting me off.

"That you're not slow, and honestly, I don't know if I want to get involved with someone that's out there."

"Well, I am who I am, and my body is mine. If I want to show it off, that's what I'm going to do. My crew told me you were too stuck up. Guess I should have listened. Come on, cuz," she said to KaydaKay. "I don't want to play."

They got in her cousin's hooptie, pumped the music up too loud, and were out. Landon looked at me with a *Why you mess me up?* expression. I told him to get in the car, and we drove off. Was I being too judgmental? Or were the standards that I wanted in a lady right on? It should not matter to me anyway. I was already involved, and I wasn't going to change that for just anything.

Sometimes I felt like a kid. I had knots in my stomach when I pulled up to my house, because

it was after my ten o'clock weeknight curfew.
It was just five minutes past ten, but with the
high-maintenance, maniac, narcissistic father
that I had, being late wasn't what you wanted to
do. All the lights in the family room were on, so
I knew I might as well buck up and get ready to
deal with his mouth.

Like a clock that chimes right on schedule
every hour, that's how much I knew my dad.
And as soon as I walked in the door, he rushed
over to my face, grabbed my collar, and shouted,
"Why you coming up in my house late, boy? Give
you a little bit of leeway and you can't show me
that you're responsible. I am so sick and tired of
you doing what you want to do, thinking you're
grown in this house ... gimme them keys!"

Of course, I was not doing what I wanted
to do. If left up to me, I'd be out with the boys.
Leo surely did not have to be home at ten. I
resented my dad because I was not really that
late. I appreciated that he was my father, and
that he was the higher authority in my life. But
he was not a zookeeper, and I was not an ape.
There could have been an accident that held me
up. My girlfriend might not have been able to

get into her house. Anything could have been a reasonable excuse for my delay. He could have asked me or given me grace.

However, he was not backing down and neither was I. My dad and I were looking eye to eye. We were standing toe to toe. At that point we were standing man to man, because I was not going to have him sock me, hit me, or push me around.

"What you going to do, Blake? You think you can take me? Got a couple little muscles on you, so are you going to come up in my face, thinking you can take me? Boy, you don't pay no bills in this house, and when I tell you to be home at a certain time, use your cell and call me if there is an issue," he said, as my irritation became slightly verbal. "What ... you gonna groan, grunt, make some mumbling sound? Boy, I'll—"

My mom just screamed out, "Stop, Brad!"

She came and stood between the two of us. She was not anywhere close to either of our sizes. She stood firm, wanting us to back away from each other.

"Brad, you know I can't take this right now. Please!"

My dad yelled, "No, I'ma show this boy he ain't grown."

"Just stop," she squealed.

My mom was crying. As her emotions started to become more intense, I realized that she was extremely upset and not just because of the brewing altercation before her. She went over, sat on the couch, and started rocking back and forth.

Knowing my mom as I did, I knew there was more to her sad demeanor. Then when my dad rushed over to her, put his arms around her, and completely settled down from tripping, I knew something was terribly wrong.

My dad held her and said, "I'm sorry, baby. I know there's a lot going on. I'm sorry. I'm just not handling all this the right way."

"You can't put more on me right now, Brad," she cried.

I did not know what they were talking about. My parents had a pretty good relationship. My dad had always been there. I never knew us to be struggling financially. We were not rich, but all of my needs were met, unlike a lot of boys I'd come to know over the years who had absentee fathers or no father at all. They were scrambling, hoping, and praying that they would eat. As much as my dad irked me, he was a faithful husband. I guess that's why I didn't want to just get with a girl. He was an excellent role model when it came to being the head of the home, and whatever had my parents so upset was starting to creep me out.

"What's wrong? What's going on? Talk to me, you guys," I said in a panic.

I did not want my dad to get upset again and say, "It's none of your business," or "It is none of your concern," because seeing my mom in tears was for sure my concern. Though my dad could be a big jerk, I knew he had not done anything stupid like cheat, misuse all the money, or start drinking. So what had her so shaken? Had she lost her job?

She was a branch manager for a bank. We moved to Georgia because she got a promotion. Maybe they had downsized and she was let go. Even if that was the case, we should be fine. My parents had always talked to me about how to be smart with money and that I could always get everything I needed because they had put some away for a rainy day. They did not believe in getting credit cards to blow up and max out. They had a couple of cards for emergencies only. It could not be a job loss freaking my mom out. If she did lose her job, certainly she was qualified enough to get another one. And even if we had to go a bit without her salary, from everything they told me, we were covered.

When my mom kept crying, I went over to the other side of her. My dad looked away and when he looked back at me, tears were in his eyes too. I was shaking with worry.

I was not an only child. I had a younger sister, Lola, who was headed to the seventh grade. She was going to be a week late starting school because she was in a summer ballet program in New York.

"Oh my gosh! Is it Lola Ivy?" I asked, calling my sister by her whole name, which we did only when we were serious. "Is everything okay with her in New York? She's not hurt or anything is she?"

"No, no, son," my mom mustered up the courage to say. "I'm so sorry to break down in front of you like this. I told your dad I wouldn't do it, and we don't know everything going on with me, so why stress? However, I haven't been feeling too well. Also, I found a lump in my breast."

I heard exactly what she said, and at that moment, it felt like I had been shot. My whole body became numb, and it felt like my heart had been shattered into a billion pieces. I had to be in a nightmare because there was no way in the world something physically could be wrong with my mom. She was a rock, always going one hundred miles per hour. I knew nothing of how PMS got women down because I never knew one moment when my mom was on or off of her cycle. She never had mood swings. She was sassy, fierce, confident, and strong. A lump. *Cancer*. It just could not be.

"No, no," I kept repeating. "No, no."

I stood up and backed away from my parents. My dad came over and held me tight. He and I both broke down. Then I pushed him away because I refused to believe something was wrong with my mom. She had to be okay. Things had to be right. There could be nothing wrong with her. I would not accept anything less.

My mom got up, wiped her face, stood beside me, and placed her arms on both of mine.

"It's going to be okay, honey. Whatever the doctor is going to tell us, it's going to be okay."

But how could it be okay if she was ill. My heart got hard. All of this was not fair.

My parents consoled each other. I grabbed my keys and got out of there. I didn't care about the consequences. It didn't matter that I knew I was supposed to be getting ready for school. I didn't care if I didn't sleep at all because I had just been hit with the worst news imaginable. My mother might have cancer, and as big, fast, and strong as I was, there was nothing I could do about her facing sickness.

As I drove like a maniac, exceeding the speed limit, driving in the median, and going around slow cars, subconsciously it didn't matter if I crashed because the thought of living this life without my mom was unbearable. If I wasn't here, that problem was solved. I guess there was something else working inside of me that calmed me down because the next thing I knew, I was in my cousin's neighborhood.

It didn't look as upscale as the one I lived in. It was late at night, and the place was jumping.

The place where I lived was like a closed mall. Brenton's area had six and seven cars in certain driveways. Some were broken down and on bricks. Even though it was night, you could see the place wasn't well kept, and maybe that's why I didn't feel sorry for people.

Though I was just a young black man, there was so much about my race I didn't understand. Yeah, my parents provided a lot for me, but I worked hard on my own. When you see people not taking care of property, being all loud and rude in the middle of the street, not moving when they see a car coming, and with no common courtesy for their fellow man, I understood why some people don't want to be around Negroes.

As I honked the horn for the brothers to get out the way, finally realizing they were so high they probably didn't understand I was trying to get around them, I felt we had to do better. Martin Luther King Jr. had a dream. He risked his life and didn't even get to see his own children grow up so that we could be about something, and I knew in the pit of my gut that he wouldn't be proud of the majority of black men: in jail, on drugs, not taking care of their families, and gone too soon.

That's when I realized I was no better. I had to figure out a way to handle my problems. Black men probably turned to booze sometimes, not only because it was cheap to get alcohol, but also because it was easy to turn up the bottle and wash away their problems when jobs were hard to find and owning much of anything was out of reach. I could only imagine how a man must feel when he couldn't take care of his family. Girls just throwing themselves at you trying to get pregnant so they can latch on to any dollar somebody worked hard to earn. I wasn't just trying to blame females. It took two to tango, and if you decided it was cool to lie down with the sista, then whatever the consequences might be, you got to take care of it. It was easy for me to understand the plight of the black man, and that let me know I should not be so judgmental.

When I pulled up to Brenton's yard, there was a whole bunch of yelling going on, and the front door was open. I quickly jumped out of my car and ran inside. My aunt's place was being ransacked. A man I had never seen before was tripping before my very eyes.

"Grab his arm, Blake!" Brenton yelled out.

Brenton held the man by one hand, and before he could chuck my aunt's lamp across the room, I grabbed his arm, and the lamp fell to the couch. The man started tugging, wiggling, and going ballistic.

"What's wrong, Aunt Val?" I called out.

My aunt was just standing there, shaking.

Brenton yelled, "I told you, Mom, don't trust him. I told you not to let him back in this house. I told you I saw him the other day around the corner, stoned."

"He needed something to eat, Brenton. I was just helping my friend. I mean, we been dating … I didn't know, but he came in here all drunk and high, Blake," my aunt started saying to me. "I was so glad Brenton came home because he was hit …"

"What? *What?* You better tell these boys to leave me alone. I'm gonna call the cops on your tail. That's what I'm gonna do. They gonna lock you up. Then what?"

"Joe, just get out of here!"

It was hard to get the man to cooperate, but Brenton and I handled it. Though he was kicking and screaming, we got him up out of my aunt's place. My cousin wasn't the starting linebacker for a 5A program for nothing. He grabbed that man by the collar like he was the dumbbell in practice and pushed him back so far he ended up falling on the concrete.

"I'm giving you this pass just once, but if I ever see you five feet in front of my house again … I'll …"

I grabbed my cousin and pulled him away from the man. When I looked back, the dude had run away. I hadn't seen my cousin upset like that ever. It was just a mess.

Brenton was breaking down in my arms so much that I could not even tell him my mom might have cancer. I had to put my hurt and pain aside and be there for not just my cousin, not just my boy, but for my brother.

"It's going to be all right, man," I said.

"He put his hands on my mom, Blake. I just don't understand why she trying to get with any old joker, man. For a hug and a kiss, for a couple dollars … Dang, man, I got to quit the football team. I got to get another job. I got to take care of my mom so she don't need nobody else to take care of her! I just got her, Blake. I just got her!"

I looked up at the perfect night sky and knew that I could not break even though I felt like I was in my own pit of doom. For my cousin's sanity ... For him to know we can get through this ... For him to know he wasn't alone ... For him to know whatever he had to do, he wasn't quitting the football team. We needed him. I had to be strong. He had to be strong. We had to keep our guard up.

CHAPTER 3

Excellence Showing

I felt like I had to be excellent, performing at my maximum best, ready to dominate, and the best QB ever seen, because I was getting ready to head to the National Underclassmen Combine—an elite football camp—in Birmingham, Alabama. My parents were going to be taking me, Brenton, and Landon. We were invited to this camp after being selected as one of the top fifty players in each position in the South. Landon was one of the top receivers. Brenton was one of the top linebackers. And I was doing my thing as one of the top quarterbacks across the states of Alabama, Mississippi, Tennessee, Florida, South Carolina, and Georgia.

Of the other top forty-nine players in our position who got invited, we did not know exactly how many would show up. However, we knew the ones who came were going to have their game faces on. I was determined to show them what I was made of.

We were leaving so early in the morning that Landon and Brenton stayed over. They were piled up on the floor in my room on two different air mattresses. I was lying restlessly on my bed.

Landon must have looked over at me wrestling and said, "Blake, man, you ain't sleep?"

"Yeah, I'm sleep," I said, hoping he would get the message that I did not want to talk.

I had a lot on my mind. Neither of them cats knew what was going on with my mom. Also, my father was still tripping. Though every part of my game was sharper in practice, I knew my dad was still not satisfied with my forty speed. Although a quarterback does not have to have super speed, I wanted to be dominant in all areas. I did not like that Brenton could bench press more than me. Yes, he was a linebacker and was supposed to be stronger; however, I still did not like it because I wanted to be superior in every skill. Landon was like lightning, and I wished I had his flash. I really wanted to get the two of them up so they could help me in my weak areas, but it was too late in terms of morning hours and too late because we were competing the next day. Where I was as a player was pretty much where I was going to stay. I'm not a whiner, but I thought it was easier to just say, "Yeah, I'm sleep," hoping that Landon would be like, "All right, man," and leave me alone.

"What about you, Brenton?" Landon asked, obviously wanting to talk.

"Tryna dose off," Brenton said, truly sounding tired.

"Y'all can't sleep like me," Landon said nervously. "I'm jittery, and I feel like my heart is gonna fall out of my chest. I don't know if I can go through with this tomorrow."

"Landon, come on, partna," Brenton said to him. "You straight, man."

"You're not the only one nervous," I finally admitted.

"Cuz, don't you trip. You are the baddest quarterback around," Brenton said, surprising me that he was that confident in my skills.

Thinking about all that was on me, I became emotional. The light from the moon shone into my bedroom. I did not even realize that they could see me wiping me eyes.

"Blake," Landon sat up and said in a caring voice. "Brenton's right. You know you gonna show out tomorrow. Dude, I don't ever think I've seen you cry. What's wrong?"

Being vulnerable, I said, "It's my mom, man."

"What's going on with Auntie?" Brenton asked, as he sat up too.

"I don't even wanna talk about it. You guys need to concentrate, and I don't want to add none of my stress to y'all."

"Fo' real, Blake, don't front," Brenton said. "You was there for me. Don't hold out. If you going through, I'm going through. What's going on with Auntie? I'ma be worried crazy if you don't tell me now. You gotta spill it. What's going on?"

"She may have cancer. There, I said it," I yelled, letting out some of my pent-up frustration.

My room got silent. Landon got up and put his arm on my shoulder. I cried harder. My cousin bowed his head. I assumed he prayed. It was good to know I had two teammates—friends, no brothers—who really felt my pain.

The next morning we were on our way to the National Underclassmen Combine. I did not want my mom coming because I did not want her stressed out, as I knew she'd be nervous for me. However, as my favorite cheerleader, she was in the car pumping us all up. I hoped Brenton and Landon would not treat her differently, and they did not, which was cool. They laughed with her, and she enjoyed that we said we were going to represent.

The three of us were a little uneasy, and we'd hardly slept, but when we stepped onto the football field in Birmingham, Alabama, and saw the massive crowd of top athletes, we knew we were ready.

My dad was more nervous than my mom. First he was in the stands. Then he was hanging on to the fence. Next he was walking the track and biting his nails. Finally he stood in the end zone where he was kicking at the dirt. The man could not stay still. But I blocked him out. I told Landon and Brenton that this was our time to shine, and if there was one thing we knew how to do, it was to take our play up another notch. The National Underclassmen Combine needed to be ready for us.

When the head coach, Coach Lot, asked us to assemble for warm-ups, we lined up across the end zone. I stood straight in front of him on the front row, and Brenton and Landon were beside me. We were jumping up and down, hitting each other in the chest, making grunting noises, and firing up everyone around us. Yeah, we were in competition with these other guys, but all of us had done something amazing to get to this level. If we had confidence and enthusiasm for each other, this would be a better experience for us all.

When stretching was over, Coach Lot came and divided us all up by position. I was no different when it came to leading the drills. I was too hard on myself when it came to the forty because I was the second fastest out of the thirty-nine quarterbacks who were in attendance. Remarkably, it was the same thing when it came to lifting the weights. I lifted 155 pounds twenty-three times. I was second to only one guy. In every other event I performed, I was the best.

When we moved to actual competition, I showed out too. We worked on three-step, five-step, and seven-step drops. My footwork was on point. All of my balls had tight spirals, and the receivers had no problem catching any of my passes. One of the toughest throws to make is the deep out route, but my arm strength made it happen for me with ease. They rotated quarterbacks in for the competition. When I was on the field, my team was able to move the ball extremely well. I had the most TDs. Coach Lot picked the top ten quarterbacks, and I was in that number.

In the afternoon when the competition was over, the Combine held a ceremony. Coach Lot stood at the front of the group and announced, "More impressive than being in the top ten in your position is being number one in your position."

I could see my dad gritting his teeth when the best linebacker was announced, and he almost ran onto the field when Brenton came forward. When he announced the best wide receiver, and Landon's name was called, my dad did a dance.

My dad yelled louder than any cheerleader I recalled ever hearing when I was named the top quarterback. My dad ran on the field and kissed me on my cheek. I was embarrassed, but I was extremely proud.

Most days he gives me a hard time, and he makes me feel last when it comes to all the other players. However, that moment when he went that extra step to let me know he was hyped that I had accomplished something really awesome, meant a ton. He showed me his love. We just hugged. Even if he grilled me on the way home, or if the next day's practice was hell, or if I should disappoint him during the seven-on-seven game that was coming up at the end of the week, I knew that at that very moment he was proud of me. Nothing could take that feeling away.

To top it all off, there was a tie for the leadership award that was given. Coach Lot announced that it was the first time in the Combine's history that the award was given to three people from one school. Landon, Brenton, and I represented the Lions with class. Needless to say, we were proud, but we were hungry. On the way home my dad took us to a steakhouse. We were full from our tummies and from his love.

Seven on seven meant that there were only seven players on offense and seven on defense. We did not really need linemen because there was no hitting permitted. It was really a passing league, and there was a bunch of talk that got around that I was chosen as the top quarterback at the National Underclassmen Combine, and I was only going into my junior year. I had been coached up for years because of my dad, but I was maintaining my dynamic status because of my skills.

We knew when we stepped off of the bus that the team to beat was Rutland from Bibb County in central Georgia. They were tough. They were mean. And they were gunning for me. When I saw the size of their linebackers, I wondered why they weren't at the Combine. Then I remembered that not only did you have to be good, but there were fees attached. The higher the level, the more money you had to pay, so some boys who were good opted not to go that route because they could not afford it. Sizing up the big gorillas in front of me, I knew some cats did not need the Combine and camps to get their play out there to college scouts.

"So all I'm going to say, Lions, is I need intensity. We're going up against eleven other teams. The team still standing at the end of the day wins the seven-on-seven tournament," my dad stated with passion.

The first three games, we breezed through. We were tired on game four. Some guys got cramps, as the heat was the biggest opponent, and it was whipping our tails.

My dad reeled all of us in and said, "When you're a Lion, you have courage. You protect what's yours. Though you're a beautiful creature, you can get mean and nasty. So dig down deep into yourselves and turn it up another notch. Matter-of-fact, what's that song you used to sing a couple of years ago? 'All the Way Turned Up.' Let's finish this thing. You guys are the best-conditioned team out here. I know it. Play like it."

Though we were struggling in the beginning of game four, we pulled through. During game five the other team was flat, and we basically won because they played so pitifully. Then we had to face the big monster, Rutland, and they were talking noise.

"Hey, Blake. I heard them boys hurt somebody in the last game. You ain't really supposed to hit like that. Don't throw up no high balls 'cause I'm not catching it. I ain't tryna get no cheap shot," Landon said, as we scouted out the other guys.

I wanted to go tell my dad exactly what I'd heard about the opponent, but he was already on it, and he called us in again, and said, "All right, I talked to the refs, and we don't have to play these guys because a couple of them took some cheap shots. One guy was ejected and can't even play in this game. So if we don't want to go, they'll call it a draw. It's y'all's choice. I already like how y'all played. I don't want anyone to get hurt. We can walk away from this thing and live to fight another day. Our season is more important. It's a few weeks away, and it's gonna be a jungle. I need all my Lions ready to roar."

We all were eyeing each other. None of us said anything. My dad took that like we were ready to pack it in and go home.

My eyes got bigger and excited, like a lion's does when he sees prey he wants to devour. "Hold up, Pops. We ain't scared. Like from your favorite movie, *The Wiz*, we're not like the lion in the beginning of the film. As a matter of fact, we got the brains the Wiz gave Scarecrow, and I know we can outsmart Rutland. We got the heart like Tinman got. We play as a team, and we're not gonna let each other down. We have the courage of a lion. They might be bigger, but they're not faster and stronger. Big doesn't always mean better. Just like Dorothy, we wanna go home. Only difference is, we're going home with the prize."

My teammates started roaring a lion's call. My dad nodded. We were ready to play.

They scored the first two touchdowns, making one TD after picking off one of my throws. Though frustrated, I did not lose my head. I kept the team motivated. The next three scores were ours. We went home champions.

On the bus my dad said, "There are lots of seven-on-seven tournaments going on around the state. Contenders wanted to be in this one because twelve dynamic teams competed—no chumps. You guys came out champions. I'm proud of you men. Proud of your hard work. It pays off. This is only the beginning. Get ready for the jungle, baby, get ready for the jungle! Y'all go out, have yourselves a good time. Take tomorrow off, and I'll see you first thing Monday morning. On three: one, two, three … Lions!"

We all roared.

"When yo' pops said we can go out, I didn't know he meant you, too," Colby, a nagging defensive back came up to me and said later, as we were about to go into a house party.

Landon had my back and said, "You need to get some skills because we were getting burned in the secondary."

Landon looked at me to join him in the roast, but I was feeling too good for the drama. Brenton laughed, letting Colby get the message that his play was sorry. I just stared at the brother.

"Don't look at me like that, Blake. My leg was hurting out there today."

"I ain't say nothing to you, man," I said with my arms up in the air, needing him to back up the accusations I did not deserve.

"I'm just saying. I know y'all ragging me because it seemed like I wasn't holding down the secondary. But I'ma be all right. I got the corner covered," Colby said, hitting is chest.

I didn't know whose house I was in. Landon said it was some party, and Brenton and I just tagged along. The place was jumping, and it didn't look too suspect. Some places I did not need to go into because it just looked like trouble, but this was a calm, peaceful neighborhood, and there did not appear to be any thugs around. I could not go in just any place. I had a rep to protect and a future to be around for.

Before I walked in, I dialed Charli's number. "Where you at, baby?" I said, wanting my arms to be around her.

We did not stay on the phone for three minutes. She was busy and quickly hung up on me. That really got under my skin. I really wanted to tell her how good I had been ballin', and I also wanted to tell her about the turmoil in my family. However, the one girl who said that she wanted to be mine kept pushing me to the side. That was not cool.

Brenton came back out and said, "Man, I don't know. Look a little suspect. I saw some

Axes in there. Landon said he straight. He can stay, but it's not our scene."

Brenton did not have to sell me. I was up for avoiding trouble. I did not want to go straight home though. I huffed.

Brenton said, "No worries, bro. After you take me home, you can go swing by Charli's place. I know you said you were gonna call her."

"She's with the doggone cheerleading squad having some swimming party."

"Let's go over there," Brenton smiled and suggested.

"Yeah, that's what I told her. She said it was just for the team, some bonding thing, or whatever."

"Oh, well, that's understandable."

"Man, whatever. I wanna love on my girl."

Brenton shook his head and walked to the car, but I didn't follow. "I know you aren't going in there. Man, let's go," Brenton said.

"I'm just gonna go and check it out for a second. Dang."

Something told me I should've listened to my cousin, but sometimes I just did not want him to think what he said was law. However, I knew I could not stay because there were not only beer bottles everywhere, there were also a couple of drug dealers in the joint giving out samples, two boys beating down some dude, and folks was making out in the main room. This one couple in particular was going at it; they needed to get a room. All of a sudden the girl pushed the guy off, and I was surprised to see Jackie's face. I immediately turned around and got out of there. I did not know if she saw me or not, and it really wasn't important.

I texted Landon and told him he needed to be out too. However, whatever he did was his business. Frankly, I was tired from carrying around my own burdens. What was going on with my mom was weighing me down. Always performing at the high level was stressing me. I was really worn out from trying to figure out Charli, because in the area of showing up when her man needed her, she was failing.

As soon as I dropped Brenton off, my phone rang. I looked down and saw it was Jackie. I frowned, thinking she had some nerve calling me after her hands were all over some other dude.

I blurted out, "Hold your breath until I call you."

I kept driving along and couldn't believe I was going home early, but there was no need in staying out when I could barely keep my eyes open. Even if I had another hour before my curfew, I was exhausted and needed to listen to my body and go rest up.

My phone started vibrating. I picked it up and saw that I had a text. I needed gas, so I pulled into the station to fill up. It was against the law to text and drive in our state. My dad already gave me the talk about being a black male and driving late at night. He told me I needed to look out for driving while black. Sometimes certain policemen give black males a hard time because of the color of their skin. He warned me not to do anything to break the law, and I'd have a better chance of making sure nothing happened. If I did get pulled over, he taught me how to be humble and not be rude so I would not inflate the situation and have tension mount.

Seeing Jackie's name, I debated on if I wanted to read Jackie's text, but the first word on my iPhone said, "Help!!!!"

My phone rang again. It was her and I answered it. "What's that about?"

Jackie did not respond because she was hysterical. She was screaming and crying. I was stunned.

"Come get me, please. I need you, please," she finally was able to say.

Knowing she was in real trouble, I said, "Where are you?"

"I'm walking outta the neighborhood you were just in. Please, come get me. Please!"

From her voice, I knew she was not faking. I filled up, got two Gatorades, paid, got back in the car, and headed back to that crazy party.

Thinking it over, I called Landon. "Dude, you still over there?"

"Yeah, man," Landon replied.

"I'm just letting you know I'm rolling back that way. Jackie called me and ..."

"Good, 'cause you can help her get outta the house."

"What do you mean help get her outta the house?"

"Some dude was coming on too strong. Her cousin KaydaKay was looking for her, and I started getting some smooches, so we jetted out. Find her, all right?"

"Jackie's already out of the house. Bye, boy," I said, hanging up the phone on my partna who was busy trying to get lucky.

I wanted to make sure he had my back just in case I needed it. I knew there were some loose cannons in the direction I was going. However, Landon had already left the place, trying to get busy.

Thankfully, Jackie was alone. I saw her on the side of the road, shaking. Quickly, I pulled over, helped her into the car, and asked her, "What happened?"

But she was talking crazy so I couldn't make out much of anything she was saying. Then I saw her torn shirt, and when I pulled into a parking lot, I noticed her eye was bruised pretty bad.

"Oh heck nah. I'm going back over there. This is crazy."

"No, no, no," she kept panting. "Just hold me, please." After about ten minutes she said, "We were dancing, and the next thing I know he had his hands all over me, and he pushed me up against the wall. He is two times my size, and he was groping me in places that were just disgusting. I was so repulsed I felt frozen, but then I got enough strength to push him off of me. That's when I saw you leaving. I know you thought I was with him, but we were just dancing. Then the next thing I know, he was tryna take it to a whole different place that I didn't even want it to go. You believe me, don't you? You *do* believe me, right? Tell me you believe me, Blake."

I wiped her tears, and I didn't let her go. I became angry. For some reason, I really wanted black men to do better, and for our whole race to act like they had some sense. For any guy to take advantage of a female was completely wrong. I went through the drive-thru and ordered Krystals with cheese. I got a cup of ice, drove around to the side of the parking lot, and put some ice in a napkin. Gently, I laid it on her face. She said ouch, but I kept the ice on and eventually it got more comfortable.

"He was holding my mouth. He wouldn't let me scream. Finally when he twisted his hand the right way, I could feel a piece of his palm. I bit it as hard as I could and kneed him. I got away then."

I tried to think of who the joker was because he went to my school. I knew seeing her all beat up that this wasn't over. I wanted to make him pay.

"When you saw me, something in your eyes let me know that you were disappointed. You told me about dressing too loose. I don't know if that's because there are some feelings that you have for me, Blake, or what. But I knew I wanted to be with you, and that guy just wouldn't let me go. When I called you the first couple of times, I just knew you weren't gonna come."

"I'm sorry," I said for making her feel dirty and alone. "I'm sorry."

I realized holding her that I did actually have feelings for her. I'd told her to cover up because I didn't want the world looking. I also did not want men thinking they could take what she was advertising.

"Just hold the ice on your eye, sit back and relax, and I will get you home. Okay?"

She grabbed both of my hands and said, "Thanks for being a gentleman. Thank you for caring. Thank you for being an example of what every guy should be."

Caring, I said, "Just hold it and relax. Don't worry about none of this."

In my mind, I was making a mental picture of what the guy looked like, because in school it was going to be on. He did not need to push on or hit on a female. I wanted him to try that junk with me. The ice was melting, and water from the ice was dripping down Jackie's shirt. She didn't move. She was relaxing, but something deep in me was rising. When I saw an indentation pop out from her shirt, it truly made me want to get to know her in every way. Jackie was kinda known for showing a little too much, and at that time I could see it all, and boy did I want to touch. Her low-cut blouse was partially open on one side, and from my view there was an excellent show going on.

CHAPTER 4

Mounting Pressure

Being in the cold, creepy hospital waiting room made me completely uncomfortable. My mom was having a biopsy to see if her lump was malignant or benign. I did not understand all the terms, but I wanted the medical folks to find out it was nothing, and that she would be okay, which I understood meant benign.

However, there was something in my parents' eyes when they looked at each other before she was taken back to have the procedure done that scared me. My dad gripped her hands really tight and kissed them, as if to say, "Whatever comes out of this whole thing, we are going to be able to deal with it." She nodded slowly and hugged him, not wanting to let him go. He found the chapel in the hospital and went to pray, but I could not move from the waiting room.

My sister was having the time of her life in New York finishing up her ballet tour. She would be back soon. But missing the first few days of school was not all that she did not have to deal with. She had no clue any of this was going on, and I guess the three of us would have it no other way. My parents tried to shield me. They didn't want me to know any of this either, but they had to reveal the truth to me after that intense fight with my dad.

As I sat in the waiting room, shivering, I wanted to be a better person. I did not think I was cocky. I just tried to be confident, but lately I knew I had not been completely right with Charli. She had no clue I had taken Jackie home. She certainly did not realize that I was lusting over someone else. I had to straighten up my bad ways. So I figured that I would call Charli so I could apologize, but it went straight to voicemail.

"Son, you all right?" my dad asked, startling me out of my thoughts.

I did not understand why he asked me that question. Of course I was not all right. My mom could be dying. However, I knew I was his man, his boy, his baller, and come what may, I was supposed to be tough, never vulnerable, and no emotion was ever allowed.

Standing up to face him, I said, "Yeah, Dad. I'm cool. You straight?"

Clearly, I could see he had been crying. His eyes were red. He had not been sleeping because he had bags under them, and it was not because he was watching film. He told me he had gone to the chapel, so I knew he wanted help from above. Why did we have to pretend like everything was okay? Why did we have to be strong?

Being the tough man I knew he was, he said, "Oh, yeah, yeah, yeah, this is all taken care of. I have no worries. I was just concerned about you. Your mom is going to be fine."

Now I do not know why he was so optimistic. He was not a doctor. We had not been given a diagnosis. My mom was not even out of surgery, for goodness' sake, but he was set on his faith. So I let him believe whatever he wanted.

"Dad, do I have to stay here?" I asked, knowing my mind was going crazy.

He said, "No, son. You got your car. We'll meet you back at the house. I don't want you waiting around, and your mom wouldn't want you stressed out."

Hearing that comment, I realized that though I told him I was okay, he knew I really was not. Ugh, too much was going on. When I got the okay to leave, I flew out of the waiting room. However, when I got to the elevator, I paced back and forth. My mom might need me. I did not want her to wake up and me not be there. I did not want her to think what she was going through was not my top priority, because it was. I simply was not as strong as I thought I was. It felt like the walls were closing in on me, like I was stuck in that elevator or something, and I could not breathe. I had to get out of there. When the elevator doors opened, I took the stairs.

As soon as I got to my car, I called Charli again. Voicemail again. When the phone rang back, I quickly picked it up, ready to hear my girl's sweet voice. However, I looked at the sleek black gadget and saw it was Brendon.

"Wassup, man?" I said with little zeal.

"I'm checking on you," he said to me, not sweating my flat tone. "How's Auntie?"

Trying to stay strong, I said, "In surgery, cuz. I don't know. This is real hard, Brenton. What if I lose her? I can't lose her."

Becoming emotional, I put the phone on speaker. I took both of my hands and firmly grabbed the steering wheel. With all my built up anger and frustration, I started shaking it. My car wasn't new, but I did not want to break it. But there was something in that whole forceful movement that made me feel better.

Brenton stayed on the phone and kept saying positive things. Before I knew it, tears were falling. He could hear me. He just told me to go ahead and let it out. I didn't feel like a wimp. I felt real, and though my cousin was not physically with me, I was not alone.

"You both will be okay. She's gonna be all right. You'll see. Why don't you call Charli, man?" he said after I calmed down.

"Tried. Girl is too busy for me."

"She'll hit you back, no worries."

"Yeah, all right," I said, as I was getting mad at Charli.

"Well, call me as soon as you hear anything."

"I will. How's your mom?" I asked, remembering the crazy dude we had to take down.

"Good, she hasn't even seen that joker anymore."

"That's good because the last thing I want to have to do is ..."

Cutting me off, Brenton said, "You don't even have to say it."

"Right, all right, man. Take care of yourself," Brenton said, as we hung up.

Brenton was right. I did need to talk to a female. They were different than guys, and though I could be transparent with my cousin, he wasn't a female. The scent of a lady, her soft smooth skin on mine, her purring voice ... I don't know ... a lady just had a way with a man.

I needed uplifting, and I knew if I called Jackie, I would not have to guess whether or not she would answer the phone. I did not have to wonder whether she would make time for me. I did not have to think I was bothering her. I knew she would pick up, and just as I believed, it happened.

"Blake, oh my gosh, you called me," she said with excitement.

"Yeah, I need to see you."

"Cool, my mom's home. You're welcome to come over. She's making plenty of fried chicken if you're hungry."

"Ask her if that's all right. I don't want to just come over."

"She standing right here. It's fine."

"All right, I'll be there in a second."

When I pulled into Jackie's driveway, I had second thoughts. I had not broken up with Charli. However, I needed her and she was not there.

"Oh my goodness. Is this *the* Blake Strong who's got my daughter all crazy?" a lady whose T-shirt was two sizes too small asked.

I could definitely see where Jackie got her ways. Her mother was not trying to be old. She was flirtatious as she smiled, winked, and felt my muscles.

"Come on in, don't be shy. Jackie told me how things went down last night, and you were there for her. I really owe you, so come on in here and get some of my food. I know how to do a proper thank you. I'm old school, but I don't look it, right?"

"Mom," Jackie called out, as it was clear she was embarrassed by her mom's antics.

She took me by the arm and led me into the kitchen. "Calm down, girl. I know you like him. You two talk. I'll be right back."

My eyes were wide open when Jackie's mom exited. Her bottom had sass. She was twitching too, hoping I looked for sure. Her mom looked like she really should be her sister.

Jackie saw me staring and confessed, "She was a teen mom. Don't tell her you think she's hot because she will be sweating you for real, thinking she has a chance. 'Round here she's actin' like she's the teen and not me."

The two of us laughed. Jackie was truly cool though. No pomp and circumstance. She was real, and I loved that we were not trapped behind a wall of politeness.

"She's cool. It's good to have somebody who you can hang with and who cares."

"I care about you," she said, as she put her hand on my cheek. "You said you wanted to talk to me. What's going on?"

"Nah, forget it," I said, suddenly wanting to man up.

Jackie would not let up. "Talk to me. What's going on?"

"It's my mom. She's having a biopsy today."

She came real close to me and hugged me. Our bodies eased down to the chair. I did not know where her mom was in the house, but when she was sitting on my lap, everything in me arose. Next thing you know, she was making me feel good as her lips met mine. If someone was to say, "Charli," I would say, "Charli who?" And could you really blame a brother?

"So wassup, man?" Leo said later that evening when I was hanging out with my boys at the bowling alley.

Leo Steele was our defensive end. He was a phenom. At six three and a half, two hundred twenty-five pounds, he had amazing speed and the longest arms, ready to wrap an opponent, plus the super strength to tackle them and keep them down—my boy was beyond a stud. However, he had lots of issues. He was not the smartest kindergartner in the class from what I heard, and now that we were in high school, he was some years behind. Since he did not like being embarrassed, he did not ask questions. So when Leo got lost, he acted as if he didn't care. To get attention, he got into tons of trouble. Other than being on me hard, my dad was on Leo even more. He told him if he had one more bout with the law, he was going to be thrown off the team.

Unlike Leo, who was really living the life: running with the bad crew and truly being a troublemaker, Landon liked to front. Landon and I both liked hanging with Leo; he was so loyal. He was my boy, but he was Landon's brother from another mother. Landon could never keep anything from him because he felt that spilling his guts would make Leo accept him more. Landon wanted to be cooler than what he was. He always told Leo everything. They were two peas in a pod. Even though Landon's dad, the good old reverend, didn't like him hanging out with Leo too much, they did.

"Sorry about your mom, man," Leo said.

"Look, I don't want nobody feeling sorry for me. I don't want this all over the team. I told Landon to keep his mouth closed," I said, looking over at the culprit.

He threw his hands up like he didn't say anything, but I knew Brenton would never talk. Brenton did not even like Leo. Landon did not have to admit it. He was guilty by default, and by the stupid look plastered on his face.

"You need to loosen up. Take your mind off all of your troubles. With all of this pressure on you, you deserve to chill out," Leo said, holding a bottle of something. "Come have a little nip with me and my boys. That's all I'm saying."

"Where we going?" I asked, needing to know what I was signing up for.

Leo looked tough and said, "Over on Watts Road."

Everybody knew Watts Road was where the freaks, the goblins, and the goons came out at night. I had absolutely no business saying, "Yeah, I'll go," but frustrated and upset, dummy me said, "Yeah, I'll go."

"Come on, you can ride with me," Landon said.

But I always had my own ride so I could jet out when I wanted to go. Also, I knew I had a curfew. I didn't need to be breaking it again. Actually, my parents were not bothering me because of all that was going on. Was not hearing any news from my parents a bad thing? Maybe they hadn't received the results yet. Either way, Leo had a good point. There was nothing wrong about chillin' with my boys. When I followed them, I called Brenton.

"Wassup, man, you got a word?" he said, being positive about my mom's prognosis.

"Nah, partner ... I'm just letting you know I am hanging out with Landon and Leo."

"Leo? Say what? Doing what? Don't tell me you are going to that lame party on Watts Road. I know you would not go there with them," Brenton scolded.

I could not say anything. There was silence on the phone. I really did not need him telling me what I needed to do. I had enough pressure on me as it was. Honestly, I was a little sick of Brenton being so darn goody-goody. My cousin was staying around his crib, making sure no more trouble came to his mom. That was admirable, but I was not like him.

"I just thought you should know," I finally said with an attitude.

Brenton and I had a rule. Always tell each other, even if it was tough, where you were going. We vowed to keep the whereabouts confidential unless one of us went missing and the other had to spill the beans. Of course, we made this pact when we were much younger, but he knew the rules. He couldn't go blabbing to my parents that I was hanging out in a shady place.

Half an hour later, Leo, Landon, and I were hanging outside because the house was too small, and too many folks were up in there. It was probably a health code violation or something with that many people, and none of us wanted to be foolin' with all our cousins.

Leo pulled out a brown paper bag, unscrewed a top, and handed the bag to me. I did not know what I was drinking. I did not care. I turned it up. Problem was I took too big of a gulp and I started choking.

Leo joked, "Easy, partner."

I looked up at him like, *Dang. Why you ain't tell me to take it slow before I drank it?*

Without me asking, Leo read my look and said, "My bad. I thought you would have took just a sip."

"You know he don't drink nothing," Landon said, grabbing the bottle and trying to be the big man and show me how it was done.

His tail choked too. The mixture was strong. Leo laughed at us both and practically dared us to try it again.

Up to the challenge and still wanting to numb my pain, I grabbed the bottle back with the brown liquid in it. This time being sensible, I took just a swallow. Leo took some. I did not like the taste at all, but I liked how it burned my insides and made me quickly shake off my frustration. I grabbed the bottle back and took another chug because it just felt like putting that alcohol in me was killing the germs of fear growing inside like bacteria. Then I started seeing double, and I was squinting because the dude who was walking toward me was the dude from the party a couple nights ago who hit Jackie. He was coming at me like he had beef with me. Whatever was on his mind, I had to let him know I wasn't having it.

So I rushed up to him and yelled, "What?"

He said, "What? Why you all up in my face?"

I pushed him, and then he came and pushed me, and it was on. "I saw you eyeing me down. What? You want some of this?"

"You better step back with yo' drunk behind," the grainy-looking dude said.

"Are you going to put your hands on a woman? Come on, it's a real man right here. Why don't you put your hands on me? Huh? Huh? I'm standing right here. What you gonna do?" I challenged.

He pulled out a gun. I was stunned. I heard something click behind me.

Leo said, "Blake, don't move."

"Wassup, Le—? Man, you gonna pull a gun out on me like that?" the dude asked.

"Shameek," Leo said, telling me the guy's name. "Put up your gun, man."

That's right. The crazy dude's name was Shameek. I could not believe I was staring down the barrel of a .357 Magnum. I was frozen, stiffer than something that had been in the freezer for months. What the heck had I got myself into? I actually did not want the guy to hit me, and I certainly did not want him to kill me.

Shameek looked at Leo and shouted, "I ain't got no beef with you, Leo. Come on, man. This is between me and pretty boy right here. When I finish with him, his mama won't even recognize him. You need to go on and let me handle this. Don't make this a war. He can't be worth that to you."

Leo laughed, letting Shameek know I was worth the risk, and said, "I think everybody needs to calm down."

"What he needs to do is take that gun out my face," I finally said after getting the courage inside to be real.

Or maybe it was the doggone alcohol talking. Maybe it was just because I was frustrated with my life. At that stupid moment, getting shot didn't scare me.

"Shut up, B," Leo said.

When Leo stepped closer to me, I was shocked to see Leo had a gun pointed right back at Shameek. Leo did not need to do anything crazy. I wasn't worried about losing my life, but I was super concerned about Leo throwing his away.

"What the heck, Leo?" I said to my friend, not knowing he was packing.

Leo said, "I invited you over my way, and I got your back. You need to go on and get in your car and take off."

"Nah, he ain't going nowhere," Shameek said, as he stepped so close that I could almost feel the steel on my temple.

"I'ma go with him, Leo. Come on, Blake. Let's go," Landon said, grabbing my shirt. He was the only one with sense out there.

"Hey, man. I ain't going to let you stand here with no gun and take him out for me. It ain't happening like that, partna, no," I said to Leo.

"Boy, will you take your butt out of here," Leo said. "Landon, y'all go."

"How you going to get home, Le?" Landon yelled, after he pulled me out to the street.

"I *am* home, fool," Leo said, as he cocked his gun to let Shameek know nothing needed to be tried.

Shameek's gun was no joke. Leo packing was a surprise too. Watts Road was where men died weekly. I could never live with myself if Leo was next to go.

However, when I got to my car, I could see Shameek and Leo were talking like boys.

Thankfully, all guns were put away. Landon handed me the bottle, and I took another gulp—this time able to handle the tough potion. I just chugged. I needed to go to the bathroom. Shucks, I just had a gun pointed in my face. I was sixteen, and that had never been my life.

"You are too drunk to drive," Landon said, trying to get my keys.

"I ain't drunk. I got this."

"All right, I'm getting my ride. Let's go before that crazy thug comes back at you."

I knew I owed Leo one. All I was trying to do was defend Jackie's honor. Turned out, I needed someone to defend me. I knew I was going to have to watch my back from now on.

When Landon turned off to go to his house, I swerved, forgetting that wasn't the way I lived. I let down the window because I needed air to blow on my face. I still was tripping over all I had just endured. While I would not want to live without my mom, with all she was going through, it would break her heart if I was gone. Not realizing the alcohol had taken over some of my faculties, my foot kept pushing harder and harder on the gas pedal. I was on the wrong side of the yellow line in the middle of the road a couple of times because I couldn't really tell where it was.

This was a problem because before I could get myself completely together, red and blue sirens were going off. I was being pulled over. I knew I was in trouble.

Talking to myself I said, "All right, Blake, be cool. You got this. You all right. You made it through your mom's operation earlier today and a gun assault just now; certainly, you can take a few words with the officer. This is no problem."

I had my hands on the steering wheel like my dad told me. My window was rolled down already so I was prepared to answer any questions. I was also ready to be polite. I had my driver's license and insurance card ready to hand to him.

The stern-faced, black officer said, "Young man, did you know you were all over the road?"

"Sorry about that, officer, sir."

"Any reason?"

"My error, officer. I do apologize."

"License and registration, please," he asked, not letting up.

I had pulled out my insurance card and forgot my registration. When I leaned over to get it out of the glove compartment, the officer pointed his flashlight into the car.

Abruptly he said, "Step out of the car, right away! Hands on the hood! Get out right now!"

I didn't know what he was talking about. Why was he tripping? I was being polite. I had not lost it. I was cool. I complied.

Then he asked, "Why do you have an open bottle of alcohol in your car? You know that's against the law? You been drinking tonight, son?"

I hung my head at that point. I was caught. I was trying to figure out how I could talk my way out of it. Football was king in our area of town, and our team was projected to do well in the state, so I prayed that the officer liked the sport. Our whole football team knew many of the cops liked working our games.

"Sir, can I be honest?" I said, trying to think of the only thing I could say. "There's a lot of pressure on me right now with this upcoming season—I play for the Lockwood Lions—and I know I'm not twenty-one. You have my license right there, and you can clearly see I'm not. But as the starting quarterback for the team, I am very responsible. I didn't realize it was in the car. It's not mine. It's a buddy's and—"

"You're making excuses now, son?" the officer grilled, like I was a piece of meat being cooked over the coals.

A little timid, I said, "No, sir. No, sir."

I did not ever want to be a criminal. I felt humiliated with both of my legs stretched apart, being patted from behind. Having my hands put in handcuffs like a thief was no picnic either.

"Officer, I said I'm sorry. Come on, man. Can't you give me a break?"

"I'ma give you a break, but I'm not going to let you get back in that car and drive."

I could not believe I was locked in a jail cell forty minutes later. Thankfully, no one was in there with me, but I was creeped out. I heard moans and groans from other tough men. Though they could not see me or touch me, I felt that this had to be a nightmare. I wanted to call my dad. My curfew had passed, but after sitting there for two hours calling the guard, and no one coming back to get me, an officer finally came back there. He unlocked my cell and then led me to a room where the officer who booked me was waiting.

I was both happy and sad when I saw my dad waiting too. "So should I just leave you here locked up? Officer Butts's son was a senior when you were in the ninth grade, so you might not remember him. He's doing me a favor by not pressing charges. But we wanted to scare you and show you what kind of trouble you could really get yourself into ... show you what the results would be if you keep on going down the path you're on. Alcohol, son?"

"I'm sorry, Dad," I said.

I wanted to tell him, "If you wanted to teach me a lesson, well, applaud yourself, because you succeeded." I thought the hospital was sterile and cold; this place smelled and was eerie too. Though I didn't ask for it, my dad wasn't the only one who gave me a lecture.

Officer Butts said, "Young man, you've got your whole future ahead of you. A lot of young brothers get into trouble because they have no positive activities. They have no parents or role models. They have nothing really going on in their heads because they haven't applied themselves in school. That's not you. People get hooked on alcohol and drugs just trying it one time. People with so much promise throw their lives away. Talk to somebody if you need to vent—*not* your teammates. They don't know any more than you do. Talk to an adult, a therapist."

"Butts, please," my dad yelled, "that boy better get a dog and talk to that. A therapist? Please ... I should ..."

My dad was clearly getting upset, and he started to charge at me. Officer Butts pulled him to the side, and the two of them talked until my dad settled down. I knew when I got in the car that my dad's anger was just going to flare up again.

"Can I go?" I said to the two of them.

Officer Butts nodded. "I don't want to see you back in here again."

"Yes, sir. You won't. Thanks," I said with a respectful tone, knowing that was expected of me.

I was not really feeling like the cop looked out for me. He could have followed me back home if he had my back and knew my dad. He didn't have to bring me down to jail to make a point. Shoot.

When I was in the car with my father, he surprised me by not saying a word. That really hurt me because I knew by his silence that he was too pissed for words. I could just hear his voice going, "All that we're going through right now... all that we're dealing with. All the stuff with your mom and you're just going to go and be stupid?" but he said nothing.

Then he finally asked, "Where is your car?"

We drove by the spot, but my car was gone. At that moment I honestly could not take it. Someone had stolen my ride. That was the icing on the cake, and the cake was already too sweet. What was I going to do now? How could he ever forgive me? How could I deal with the mounting pressure?

CHAPTER 5

Man Up

Why are you all so lazy today? It is like I'm coaching a bunch of girls. I can go get the cheerleaders, and they will give a better effort than you guys are. Everyone on the line. Now!" my dad shouted out to the team at practice.

Leo grumbled, "I don't know what's with your dad, but he got the wrong one on the wrong day."

Before I knew it, my dad was all in Leo's grill. He grabbed him by the collar of his practice jersey. Then my dad pinned him up against the fence.

My dad screamed, "Steele, you got something to say in my practice? Leo, you gonna try to smart mouth me in front of my players? You don't want to do what I say? Let's be clear, son. You got the wrong one on the wrong day. Get off of my field!"

"But, Coach, I was just playing," Leo pleaded, reaching out for my dad's shirt.

My dad frowned at Leo's gesture and walked away. He did not turn around. He walked over to the majority of us, and everyone knew my dad was on fire.

Our furious and fuming coach yelled, "Didn't I say line up? Are y'all dumb? What kind of grades are you all going to get this year? Because you know if you don't hold down a two-point-five, you are ineligible. And for *my* team you better have a two-point-seven-five. If not, you will be like Leo Steele ... off my team."

Leo jogged over to my father and said, "But, sir ... what? You're saying I'm off the team for good? I just ..."

Landon and I jogged over to Leo and tugged him away from my dad. He didn't need to press the issue right now. Certainly my father did not mean for good. Being real, Leo was too good of a defensive end for my dad to do without all season.

The grade issue was a concern though. Leo had a 2.49 GPA, and Dad was bending his 2.75 policy to let Leo play. At that moment, my boy needed to settle down. However, Leo was making a big fuss pulling away from the two of us. He was really forcing the issue with our irate coach. The brother needed to settle down.

"What's up with your pops?" Leo said loudly, as his hands went up and down in the air.

"You better hush and calm down," I told him.

Leo shouted back, "Calm ..."

I went up to Leo and whispered in his ear, "Man, you know my dumb dad just needs to calm down, come on, man."

"Uh-uh, he ain't taking football away from me." Leo desperately did not want to leave the team. "I wasn't the only one talking. I knew he didn't like me," he accused.

Landon pushed his boy and said, "Man, just chill. Go to the locker room. Dang."

Leo turned to me and pitifully voiced, "If I don't have football, Blake ..."

"You ain't gotta worry about that, man," I said calmly, as I placed my hand square on his shoulder.

I knew I didn't have a good relationship with my dad, and it was hard for me to talk to him, but for real, there was no way I was going to let my dad's little outburst be definitive. It just was not going to go down like that. Leo was more than my friend, he was my brother. If my dad knew just how much he had my back last night, he'd be kissing his tail not kicking his butt.

However, I did not want to deal with my dad because obviously something was really wrong. It was like he'd lost one of his contact lenses and his vision was blurred. What was he seeing that was so wrong with our practice? Our effort wasn't piss-poor. As the captain, I would not have allowed that. I knew I was not the coach, and he could see all from the tower where he stood. But from my view, we were pumped up. We were pushing each other, and we were executing drills. So what the heck was my pop's problem?

Old Coach Grey—a nice, white gentleman—handled our defense. He came up to Landon and me and said, "You two go on out there and get back with Coach Strong. I've got Leo. Everything's all right. Just calm down."

"Nah, you just don't know what's going on with me, Coach," Leo huffed. "He can't take football away."

I knew Leo lived in the projects. I knew he was not around the best environment. I was aware of the fact that he probably had a mark and would be taking a lot of heat because he stood up for me. I was sure word had gotten around, and his neighborhood crew was going to jump him for stepping into my beef. Leo knew that too, and he still stood up. He was that strong.

So something was really going on with him that had him breaking down about needing football so much. He and I were going to have to talk soon. He was looking at me like, *You gotta help.* Landon was tugging on me to get back out there with my father. Coach Grey shooed us away, even though I wanted to stay.

When I got back to the field, my dad was going off even more. He needed to take a laxative or something and get the crap out of his system. He was acting constipated or something. The team looked at me to help.

Finally, when the team started doing suicides, I approached him. "Dad, can we talk? Please?"

My dad did not move, and his body language said, *If you don't get the heck out of my way, I won't have a son.* He always encouraged me to stand my ground and be a leader. So taking his advice, I did not move.

Instead, I took my chances and said, "Look, Dad, I'm the captain of this team. I know you're the coach, but it's my job to protect these guys. You're working us for no reason. I don't want you to lose this team, and we've got great momentum. We work so hard for you, but that's only if you care back. We're human. What's wrong?"

"Come on, son. Come on. To the side of the field house right now," my dad yelled, as he threw down the clipboard.

He yelled at the other coaches to make sure the players were being pushed. He added thirty more reps to the twelve that we had to go. My team looked like they were about to pass out, but my lunatic father did not care.

When we got to the shade the field house provided, I was ready for him to smack me, hit me, sock me, take me down, something. Actually, what he did struck a chord. My father started breaking down. The toughest man I knew could not pull himself together. I had seen something similar to this one other time, and that was when my mom told me she found a lump, and I thought my dad was emotional then. So it could only be one thing for him to be breaking down this dramatically. My parents hadn't told me the biopsy results. He did not even have to say it because I knew she had cancer.

"No, Dad, no," I said, as I fell to the ground and started banging my fist in the dirt.

Seeing my pitiful display, my dad knelt down beside me, helped me up, and held me in his arms. He did not tell me I was wrong. He also did not say she was going to be okay.

He merely said, "I'm sorry, son." He repeated those words over and over again. At that point, we were two men down.

"We're gonna be okay, son. Everything's going to be all right," my dad said only to appease me after time passed.

"Why don't you go home? I know your mom would love to see you. I'll be there a little later on. I'm gonna finish up football practice, coaches meetings, and check out some film."

I went in the locker room to get my things to leave. Leo was sitting on the bench rocking back and forth. He stood up when he saw me. I guess I looked more shaken up than he thought I should.

"I don't want to talk right now, Le," I said to my friend. "And everything's all right with you and the team. Get on out there and show my dad what you are made of."

Leo had hope in his eyes but was scared to fully believe. "How you know?"

"Just trust me. It wasn't you," I said, reassuring my boy.

Leo asked, "Then what's wrong with you? Talk to me, Blake. You know I'm here for you, right?"

"Oh, of course, man," I said, remembering when he stepped up to that thug Shameek who put a gun to my face.

Even though Leo was really concerned, I was too upset to vent. I put my hand in the air, motioning for him to back off. I then went over to my locker and got my stuff to jet out.

"Thanks, man. Thanks for talking to your dad."

I knew I was supposed to talk to Leo about what was going on in his world, but I was too upset about what was going on in mine. But Leo's blow up, emotional outburst, and all the drama he displayed when he found out my dad was not going to let him play was too big of a deal. I could not let it go in good conscience.

Something more had to be going on, so I asked, "Leo, what's up with you? Man, you were almost crying."

Leo said, "We are getting kicked out of the apartment again. A lot is going on with my mom. I just need the stability of football, that's all."

I could dig what he was saying. When your world is upside down, football is a violent game that brings peace—very weird but true. Leo was saying he needed to belong to something. I did not like hearing that Leo was also have family problems. Over the two years I had known him, he had moved six times. Once he was in foster care, and he ran away from the family because he said he was being abused. We never talked about what was done to him, but I knew it was deep. Before that, he had pep in his step. Leo was a happy person. After that, he was grumpy and crass. If football was a bright spot in his life, it needed to stay.

At that moment, I needed a bright spot too. The bottom fell out for me, and I was not going to be no good for nobody else, including my mom, until I got me together. So ignoring the fact that Leo wanted to help fix me, I headed out. Once in my ride, which had made it safely back home after my arrest, I quickly reached over, picked up my cell, and dialed Charli. I felt hearing her voice would stabilize my spinning life.

"Hey, Blake. I miss you, babe," my girl said in an excited tone, sounding like the Charli I cared about.

"I *need* to see you. Where are you right now?" I asked, exposing my desperation.

Sounding less excited, Charli said, "I'm at cheer practice."

"Well, can I see you real quick before it starts? I just need to talk to you about something," I said, needing to hold her and wanting to be with her.

"Don't you have football practice right now?" she asked, seeming to want to give me an excuse.

"No, I'm leaving. Can we meet up? Or I can stay here at the school and go to your practice, and we can talk afterwards," I said, helping her figure out a way to fit me into her schedule.

"Blake, come on, you know that'll be a distraction. All my friends will be looking at you, and my coach will not allow it. Coach Woods wants us to win the state title just as badly as your dad wants the state football title to be yours."

She was really starting to upset me. I was going out of my way, trying to figure out a way to connect with her. I told her something heavy was going on, and she did not even ask what. She was into something else, and I know she was all fired up about being the captain of the cheerleading squad. Woo-hoo. Was it selfish of me to want a little attention? She was going on and on about I don't know what, because at that point I wasn't even listening. My mom had cancer, my heart was broken, and I needed someone who cared. Clearly, Charli was not it. No matter how much I wanted her to be my girl, she could not fulfill my needs. Now it was time for a brother to move on.

I drove without thinking. I passed the place where I got stopped by the police. I remembered being in jail again and how awful that felt. I remembered my car not being there when my dad brought me back to get it once he got me out of jail. However, he was messing with me because when I got back home my car was in the driveway. My nutty father had it towed just to mess with me. He succeeded because I was mad.

I drove around wondering what my life was going to be like without my mom. She hadn't passed on or anything. Although I knew almost nothing about cancer, I did know it was nothing to play with. My sister could not cook. My dad could not cook, and I couldn't cook. So how would we eat? My sister could not clean. My dad could not clean, and I couldn't clean. So how would we take care of ourselves? My sister could not wash clothes. My dad could not wash clothes, and I couldn't wash clothes. What would we wear? My sister did not understand me. My dad didn't understand me, and I didn't understand myself. How would I stay sane? The more I kept thinking about life without my mom, the more I was depressed.

Before I knew it, I was in front of Jackie's house, and I called her cell. "Hey."

"Hey, you," she uttered with excitement.

"Well, what are you doing?" I said. "I was just driving and wondered if you were busy?"

"I was just relaxing. Nobody's home. I'm chilling," Jackie said in a sultry voice.

Too excited, I said, "I'm in front of your house."

"Come in. I'm not dressed. I just got out of the shower, but I would love to see you," she teased.

It took me all of one minute to get to her door. When she opened the door, my tired eyes opened real wide. A skimpy towel clung to her obviously naked body. When she hugged me and the cloth dropped, I felt her fine body up against mine. I realized I was in trouble. As our lips touched and we made our way to her bedroom, I thought that maybe trouble was not such a bad thing.

I knew it wasn't going to be easy to break up with Charli, and I did feel bad when she caught me at that party with my arms around Jackie. I was not trying to be a player or intentionally hurt her. It just worked out that way. Thanks to my big-mouth cousin who let her find out where

I was, it all blew up, and Charli was broken. Even though she caught me with someone else, she was pleading with me to stay her guy. That was not the Charli I knew. Honestly, that was not the Charli I could respect. Bottom line was we'd been struggling for the last couple of weeks to connect, and our relationship was over long before I just told her we were through.

"I would say I'm sorry," Jackie said, as we walked, intertwined, back into the party together. "But you should be with who you want to be with."

"Yeah, I'm straight," I said, kissing her full on the lips. "What we have is working for me. No strings or rings, just fun!"

The fun ended when I felt an intense shove on my back. My first thought was that it was the thugs from around Leo's way. However, when I turned around, it was my cousin who was heated.

"How come you treat her like that, man? Charli really cares about you, and you just break her heart? Telling her to get the hell away from you like y'all never really had anything," Brenton blurted out, clearly showing his hand.

It was no secret that he liked Charli, so I let him vent. When he shoved me the third time, I pushed him. It was on. The two of us were tussling in some stranger's house. I was not trying to break anything. I was not trying to hurt Brenton. I was not trying to cause a scene, but it did feel good punching him. Actually, it felt good getting punched too. So much was wrong, but the violence felt right. I had all that pent-up hostility and anger. Though Jackie made me feel better in one way, I still was pretty messed up about all that was going on with my mom. So scrambled was my brain that I could not even go home.

"Man, what are y'all doing?" Landon said, as he came in and broke us apart.

We were going at the blows pretty intensely. Leo put my hands behind my back. My boys stepped in and helped us not kill each other.

I grabbed Jackie's hand, and said, "Let's go."

Wiping my bloody nose, she jerked her hand back and said, "Some of my girls are here. I can get home. Maybe you need to be alone. Just go."

I was not going to argue with her. I threw my hands up, and I was out. I had never fought Brenton before. I truly hated that it had to come to that. I could only hope that he'd forgive me. Jackie must've thought I had been a jerk to her too. We'd had an intimate moment, and now I walked out on her. I was smart enough to know that I was not really supposed to leave. She wanted me to chase her, but I didn't have it in me. I was broken, but hopefully my nose wasn't; it felt awful. My world was pretty tumultuous.

The last place I wanted to go was home, but that was where I drove straight to. My dad's car was not there, but my mom's was. When I walked into the house, I tried to head away so she could not see me.

I must have appeared worse than I felt because she said, "What in the world?"

"It's nothing, Mom. A door just hit my face," I said, looking away.

"A *door*? And I'm supposed to believe that. Come here, boy. Sit down," she said, as she went to the bathroom, came back with a cold rag, and told me to hold my head back. "What is going on with you? Jail, hanging out all hours, now fighting? This isn't like you, son. Your sister comes back tomorrow, and I need you to be strong."

At that moment I took the rag and said, "Mom, how can I be strong when you might be leaving me? How can I be strong when I know I might not have the person who loves me more than anything around? How can I be strong when you've got cancer? Come on, Ma, tell me, seriously? Knowing that you're dealing with all that you got going on, you really expect me to be strong. If I lose you …"

"Shhh," she said, as she put her fingers to my lips and held me. "Your dad has been going through this too. He's a football coach. He deals with big, mean boys. He tells them to be tough at all times, but he doesn't know how to deal with a little illness either. Cancer's not gonna beat me. I'm going to beat this disease."

"Ma, you're just saying that because you want me to be okay. It doesn't matter what you want, cancer has a mind of its own."

"No, son, I've been doing a lot of research. When you're going through this disease, you must believe that you can beat it. A patient must want to believe it. I certainly have a good reason to want to live. I've got a son who I love and who's doing amazing things. The clashing is for the football field and not the person you got in a fight with. That's not you. Going to jail, that's not you. And letting all these girls do who knows what to my son who was taught values, that's not you. I'm not going anywhere. I need to be here for you," she said to me with a penetrating glare. Then she cradled my face in her hands and said, "But if I'm not physically here … I need for you to be here for your sister and your father because between the three of you, you're the strongest. You don't just wear a Lions' jersey on Friday nights, you are a lion through and through. You have tremendous courage, so quit making stupid decisions, quit drinking, quit whining, and quit tryna work that thing in your pants."

"What you talking about?" I said, wondering if she knew this was the day her little boy became a man.

My mother said, "I know when you're getting too big for your britches. I'm your mom. Quit fighting. Quit being so grumpy. And quit crying. Be the Blake that I'm proud of. Man up."

CHAPTER 6

Broken Soul

Oh my gosh, you guys. I had so much fun in New York! It was the best. I got to go to the opera. I danced with some of ballet's finest, and at my performances I got standing ovations. You're looking at a rising star. Can I go back right now, Mom? Please?" my sister Lola boasted and begged.

My sister had not been on Georgia soil two minutes, and she was already talking about going back. We had picked her up from the Atlanta airport, and she kept repeating herself about how great everything was for her in New York. She didn't just say it a couple times. She kept saying it over and over and over, as if she was some broken record, and that was all she could say. Never once did she ask, "How was your summer, Blake? Dad, what's going on in your world? Mom, are you okay?" Nope, none of what was happening to us even entered her mind, and it was probably for the best.

My dad did not want Lola to know all that was going on with my mom, but my mother insisted. However, Lola was so into herself she thought that when we went to Pascal's, an upscale restaurant near the Georgia Dome, that the nice dinner was all about her. I wondered if my parents were going to stop her from talking, but they let her continue to ramble. I guess they thought that if she was extremely happy, the blow she was going to receive when she found out her world was not as solid as she thought would be cushioned. We ate our appetizers, our salads, and our entrées. Heck, we were practically through dessert.

I finally said, "Are y'all going to just tell her?"

My dad looked at me like he wanted to whack me upside my head. I was remembering the fact that my mom told me she wanted me to man up. My sister needed to know.

"Why are we prolonging the inevitable?" I asked.

"What are you talking about, Blake? Tell me what?" Lola questioned, finally getting that this evening out had more to it.

My dad looked down. My mom's eyes watered. Then my sister nervously put her hand to her mouth.

She shouted, "Oh my gosh. You're not getting a divorce or anything like that are you?"

She had not been home a day, and we could tell she was much more dramatic now than before she went to the Big Apple. She did not even let my parents explain. She just believed her own scenario and played it out in her mind.

"Because then that means I'll have to choose which parent I want to live with. Dad, I can't stay with you because you'll never let me date. Mom, I can't stay with you because you won't take me shopping enough. In the event of a divorce, I don't know what I'm going to do. You guys have to work this out. Divorce is not an option," she ranted, getting on everyone's nerves at the table, especially mine.

"Okay, okay, Lola. Hush, honey," my mom finally said. "It's not our relationship—"

Cutting our mom off, Lola demanded, "Well, what is it, Mom?"

My mother looked away as the tears started falling faster. My dad rubbed her back. I wanted to hug the cancer away.

"Lola, while you were gone, your mom had not been feeling that well. She's gone through a few tests and it looks like um,…" my father paused still not wanting to explain, "that she's been diagnosed with breast cancer."

"No!" my sister screamed out dramatically, though this time I knew her emotions were real.

Lola got up and hugged my mom. They both cried right there in the restaurant. I realized the waiter was staring, and a couple seated at the table next to ours was teary. People were looking on, and I saw in their faces that they were sympathetic to us. The manager discreetly delivered the check.

Nothing could be said to make Lola feel better. Telling her did not make the disease worse, and as annoying as my sister was when she was all cheery, I would have given anything to see her smile endlessly like that again. During the entire ride home, there was no joy in the air. There was no happiness to be breathed. There was no glee passing from one person to another. We were all somber.

I knew my mom loved playing board games. Mrs. Strong was the family game-night queen. If it wasn't Monopoly, she wanted to play Sequence, Chinese checkers, or Taboo. She told me she needed me to step it up and make sure I held her up so she could get through this. I knew this whole ordeal was getting my dad down in a way I could not imagine. My sister was as fragile as a flower in a hurricane. Clearly, she was not stable.

As soon as we got home I knew I needed to lighten the mood. I said, "Game on! Mom, last I remember me and you beat Dad and Lola in spades. She's back home; let's beat them again."

Just that challenge made my dad step up to the plate and grab the cards. "What? Lola and I always hold it down. You and your mom get ready for a spanking. Baby girl and I are going to beat you guys."

My dad started shuffling the cards. Lola was unsure. My mom put her arm around her.

My mom looked at her sad daughter and said, "I know you're not going to take sympathy on me. You're dad's talking trash. Think he's right, and you guys can beat us? It would mean a lot to me, baby, to play."

They hugged and we played. We had so much fun laughing as a family, not thinking about sickness, disease, or things out of our control. We only focused on each other and what was important, and that was family. If we were intact, we could battle anything. The best football team doesn't just win the Lombardi trophy because they are lucky; they win because they are a well-trained unit, and so was the Strong family, a strong family and tougher than ever.

My sister and I had a Jack-and-Jill bathroom we shared. I had gotten so used to going in without knocking that I actually forgot she was home and just barged in. I caught her crying.

I put my arm around her and said, "It's going to be okay."

Sobbing, she asked, "How do you know it's going to be fine? Mom's got cancer."

"Because she told me, come what may, we're going to be fine. And you've got your big brother here. You're not going to have to worry about nothing," I told her, and I believed every word.

She buried her head in my chest, and I knew whatever it took, I was going to make her happy again. I loved Lola and she loved me. My mom needed us to be strong for my dad. After she was cried out, she stepped back and looked up at me.

I said, "Aw, it's going to be okay. You know that, right?"

She nodded. "Thanks, Blake. Because of you I can sleep tonight. Because of you I have hope. Because of you I'm not broken. Thanks, big bro."

We had a bus ride ahead of us. Then it was time to suit up and play. Though it was just a scrimmage we were traveling to, we knew it was an important game. Word would be out around the metro Atlanta area whether we were punks or players based on the game's stats. My dad seemed like a whole different person. He was real melancholy, laid back, and not over-the-top excited, and the team fed off of his gloomy mood.

Our starting running back, Wax, was the only one talking junk. "I'ma have two thousand yards this season. No defender is going to be able to hold me back. I'm holding on to all of the balls, not putting nothin' on the ground. First-team All-American, baby. Look for the name Jason Waxton. That's wassup."

Jason, that was his name—not that I was wracking my brain trying to figure it out—but I really didn't know his name. I was tired of his bragging about all he was going to achieve without anyone's assist on the team. No kicker was talking about how many field goals he was going to score or what field position his kicks were going to put us in. No defensive lineman was talking about sacks. No linebackers were talking about force fumbles and tackles. No DBs were talking about interceptions, though we really did not have anybody in the secondary anyway. Actually, we were weak at safeties and corners. The whole team, except for Wax, wasn't saying a word. Landon, who loved to talk junk, was silent. Tuning out Wax, it was too quiet.

Wax wanted everyone to stare at him. He liked to try and showboat. I was sitting in the back of the bus, and I knew I had to lead them.

So I stood up and said, "Look, I know Wax is irritating." He looked over at me like I said something wrong. "But he's keeping it real. He's trying to do something big this year. You got to be hyped if you're here to win. I'm not going to play with a bunch of scrubs, so let's get out there and hit somebody, block somebody, run, catch—"

And someone yelled out, "And throw, punk!"

I shouted, "Oh, you ain't got to worry about that, partner. I got mine."

Two hours later we were coming out of the locker room ready to take on our Fulton County opponent. It was a new school with state-of-the-art equipment. Word was they could throw down.

Before we ran out on the field, my dad grabbed my facemask and said, "I know you got a lot on your mind, son, but let's go do this. You talked a good game on that bus, but can you back it up?"

"Yes, sir," I said, jogging to the sideline.

We won the coin toss and elected to receive. After the special teams play positioned us on our own thirty-yard line, I knew I had seventy yards to take the ball down the field. On the first play from the line of scrimmage, I moved back and held the ball as I waited for Landon to get into position. Finally, when he looked back, I threw a bomb pass to him just as I got nailed by the other team's big, nasty lineman. Landon was fifty yards down the field. He was perfectly positioned to run in a touchdown after the catch. However, the ball went straight through his hands.

A linebacker from the opposing team got up in my face. "I almost had you sacked."

"I'm a little too quick for you, bro. Better lay off the greasy food," I said, pointing to his round stomach.

I could not believe Landon missed a perfectly thrown ball. He was taking his time getting back to the offense. When we got to the huddle, I went off.

"Dang it, Landon. You almost got me killed with you not turning the route quick enough. You knew the play. Execute and run, doggone it. What? You got grease on your hands? Catch the ball. Freaking idiot."

I looked over at my dad, and he called a running play. I could've screamed. I knew that's what they were going to expect but being obedient, I handed the ball off to Wax. Unlike the smack he talked about not dropping the ball, as soon as the defender knocked him down, the ball was out. Thankfully, I scrambled to recover it.

"Dang. What I got to do? Play all the positions? I guess I got dumb and dumber on my team today," I said when we got back to the huddle. "I got to be the quarterback, the lineman, and the running back too. Can y'all handle anything? Shucks!"

"Just throw me the ball," Landon yelled, clearly annoyed with me when he needed to be upset with himself.

I looked over at my dad. Thankfully, at third down and ten yards to go, he called a passing play. I nodded and smiled. That was what I was talking about. This way Landon and Wax could run a short route, and I'd have two options of throwing a short dump pass. However, before I could throw the ball in the air, the same linebacker who had talked junk a couple of plays earlier knocked me on my tail. His big body would not get off of me, and everything in me was hurting, especially my shoulder.

Unfortunately, it was my right shoulder, and that was the arm I threw with. I felt like my world was over. Like everything I worked for meant nothing. Like all my dreams were gone and dashed in an awful second. I had opened my mouth about Landon and Wax not giving full effort, but I was the one lying there helpless. My teammates rushed over to me. Tears filled my eyes as I knew my season was gone.

I yelled like a loud cheerleader, "I broke it. My bone is shattered."

The home team was responsible for the paramedics. Their trainers came out onto the field with the emergency folks and the gurney. My dad, Coach Grey, and our trainer were out on the field too.

"Just relax, Blake. Quit fighting the pain, son," my father said, holding my left arm still.

I kept pounding and pounding and pounding it in the ground. My dad grabbed my fist and made sure it did not move.

I could not believe this, and as I was being carted away I heard Waxton say to the offense, "That's what he gets, non-supportive self. Now who's on the ground, acting like a b—"

Landon cut him off and said, "Dang, man. He's hurt. You got to go there?"

Wax fussed back, "You should want to. He was saying you ain't got no skills. He's supposed to be your friend, and he talks to you like he's the doggone coach. Well, Mr. All That might as well get used to not being in the spotlight. He'll be on the sidelines."

At that moment I realized I had been over the top. I should not have been so cavalier with them. I could not tell my teammates, who I needed on my side, anything hurtful and unnecessary.

My dad was standing beside me as I was helped on to the gurney. The paramedics started asking me questions and checking me out. For him it was like adding insult to injury. I knew this was more than he needed right now. Feeling the pain in my shoulder, I knew this was more than I needed too. Half or all of my season would be gone with a broken shoulder. It was more than I could bear.

I saw all my dreams disappear before my crying eyes. I was devastated, knowing that an injury to my throwing arm could ruin my future. The dream of me having a break-out junior season and attracting major college scouts, was gone. The chance of being offered entry to several D1 college camps next summer vanished. The opportunity to start my senior season listed as a first-team All American was snatched away. Signing a D1 college scholarship in my senior year and having the opportunity of playing on Sunday nights at a D1 school was not in my favor.

As they were starting to wheel me off the field, I moaned, "I'm sorry, Dad. I'm sorry."

My dad said, "Injuries happen, son. You were playing your hardest. I'm not mad at that. Son, if you broke your arm, man, ... seems like you would be in a lot more pain."

"Look like he's not as tough as the rest of us if he can't take a little stinger," Leo called out, ticked with me too.

None of my boys walked up to me to make sure I was okay. Though Landon had my back a little when the dude tried to call me out, I knew he was salty with me because he did not make sure I was all right. Getting rolled off the field of play seemed to take forever. The paramedics started messing with my arm again, and I screamed that I couldn't move it. I knew something wasn't right with it, but when my dad came over and popped me in the head, I was actually glad to hear him give me hope.

My dad said, "Boy, it is not broken."

"It's not, Dad?" I tried to get up but I couldn't.

"Nah, but it's badly sprained. What's hurting you is the initial shock," the paramedic said, as he put some ointment on it and wrapped it up.

My dad jogged back over to the team, and they continued the scrimmage.

"How long am I going to have to be out?" I asked the guy working on me.

"Your dad wants me to take you to the hospital and x-ray it anyway, but I feel pretty confident you can play in two to three weeks, probably, if my diagnosis is right. I'm not a doctor though. I'm just a paramedic, but I think you're going to be all right. I was watching you too, man. You got a pretty good arm. You were balling during warm ups and those first couple plays. If that one cat would've caught the ball, y'all would've had a TD."

Then I immediately thought about how mean I was to Landon, breaking him down, making him feel like he was a scrub. Now I was out of the game and on my way to the hospital and not even able to watch. I was the one who needed help.

When I got to the emergency room, my mom was there. Here she was going through her own thing, but she was there for me. It was just another sign that I needed her in my life.

"Baby, are you okay?" my mom said, rushing up to me.

Trying to calm her I said, "Mom, I could've walked in here. I'm all right. My arm isn't broken. The paramedic thinks I'm going to be able to play in a couple of weeks ..."

"We better make sure you're fine first! I don't want to hear nothing about football from you or your father. Let's get you well first!"

"Where's Lola?"

"She's at the house. She had a ton of catch-up homework to do from missing her first week of school. She wanted to come, but when your dad said he didn't think it was that serious, I told her she'd see you at home. She was worried about her big brother. I'm actually happy to see you two so chummy. Thanks, Blake," my mom said, saying more than the words she spoke.

When we were waiting for them to x-ray my shoulder I said, "Mom, it was my arm."

She rubbed my brow and said, "I know. You must have been scared, baby."

"Yeah, I thought it was broken. I know the guys are ragging on me, but it hurt so bad at first that I just knew it was shattered. Mom, what would I have done if my arm was broken?"

"Son, listen to me, and I want you to understand this. I know you and your dad put a lot of emphasis on football. And you're good at it, son, you are. However, that's not all that you can do. Football takes an awful lot out of people. Your dad wants to coach college ball and maybe one day professional football. It takes a lot to get to those levels, but he has a great track record and played in the NFL. This game is just *not* that simple, and it is *not* everything."

"I don't want to be a coach. I want to be an NFL player."

"I know, son, but so do a whole bunch of other little boys out there. Particularly little black boys thinking the only thing they can do is get out there and run. *My* son has options."

"I know, Mom. I'm smart, and you've always told me I can do whatever it is I want to do. I want to play. If that's taken away from me, I don't have nothing else," I said passionately.

The nurse came in and said, "Ma'am, we're going to go ahead and take his x-ray now. If you don't mind, please wait in the waiting room."

"No problem," my mom said to her.

After the results were in and it was confirmed that my arm was not broken, the doctor recommended that I didn't practice for a week. For a guy like me who lived, breathed, slept, and ate football, how was it going to be possible not to train?

When I got home, I did not have one phone call from my boys. I had gotten hurt, and no one made sure I was okay. Looking back over how I treated everybody, I knew I was too harsh. I had my own issues, which I took out on all of them. I was supposed to be a leader. I was supposed to show them how to care. They should not want to just pick up and move on without me.

The next day at practice I did a little physical therapy with the trainer. My team was doing their thing, going through drills, working out, and running; the last person on any of their minds was me. I did not like being alone. Not because I couldn't handle it, but because I was supposed to be with my teammates. I guess they were going to show me better than they could tell me that I had been a jerk. I was getting their message loud and clear.

Jackie hadn't even called—probably because I hit it. I hadn't even talked to her since the night of the party. Having to look inward was hard; however, I had to face the fact that I was a jerk in so many ways. Ever since the day my sister came home, I knew she was having a hard time dealing with my mom's news. We bonded that first night, but I hadn't asked her anymore about how she was coping. Yeah, I loved to pass judgment on other people. Looking in the mirror, I needed to work on *that* guy and fix his broken soul.

CHAPTER 7

Way Maker

Son, let me tell you, I have seen you at practice the last couple of days looking like you lost your best friend. I know you hate not being able to get out there because you've been injured. Also seems like something else has you down. From what I hear from Brenton, the team feels like you got the big head," my dad said, as we sat in his office after practice. "But here's the thing, I probably deserve to share some of the blame for who you are. I blame myself. I have always insisted that you have high standards. I never want you to apologize for that. You are blunt, and I think as a leader you need to let people know when they're slacking. You think you're the best, and I've always taught you that you are. A lot of these men didn't grow up that way. That's not in them. When they see someone who's confident, they take it as cocky. Maybe the scales for you might have got tipped in the wrong direction," he added. "I'm not saying your head didn't get inflated when you threw down in the seven on seven, and you went up there at the Combine and got the honor of being one of the top ten quarterbacks in the South. You have been doing some things. Legitimately, you have bragging rights. Just remember that does not mean you actually have to go brag. You know what I'm saying?"

"Yes, sir," I responded quickly, knowing that I had been doing a lot of self-reflection on my own.

"But I never had to motivate you. You always had that drive, that tenacity, and that *I'm going to make it happen!* spirit. If you find out a way to pass that on to your teammates versus pointing out what they've done wrong, then maybe that's the missing ingredient you need to soar. You know what I mean, son?"

"Yes, sir. It's been over-the-top hard. Not just you pushing me, but you're right, the pressure I put on myself is tough to live up to. Now all the stuff with mom … me being injured … took me over the edge, I guess. I have taken a couple of steps back, Dad. Though I'm the leader of this team, I'm not the team."

He smiled and nodded. "Go make them understand that. Your mom has got her first radiation treatment today."

Heading out of my dad's office, a few of the guys were finishing their showers. Some were already dressed. I wanted to catch folks before they headed out.

I yelled out, "Can I have everyone's attention?"

"No!" somebody yelled.

I said, "I deserved that."

And they were going on their merry way when Landon blocked the exit and said, "Stay y'all. Our quarterback is tryna tell us something. Dang."

Leo and Brenton also got people to sit. Wax wanted to leave, but I gave him a sincere stare, and he leaned up against a locker and motioned for me to talk. When they all huddled around, I knew it was my time to be transparent and speak from the heart.

I said, "I just wanna apologize to you guys for being a jerk. Telling you we're not gonna be anything wasn't called for. Calling a few of you names was totally unacceptable. Thinking that I was the best thing—and the only thing—this team had going for itself, is far, far, far from the truth. I don't wanna admit this, but I guess I'm my dad's son."

"Strong," a freshman yelled out.

"Strong," a lineman repeated.

"Strong!" three different players yelled in unison.

"I just want to say, watching you guys lately, I understand that we're all gifted. We are a phenomenal team when our skills are put together. I want to lead you guys again, and it's not because I'll be throwing the ball and calling the plays. No, I want to lead by having your respect. I know that has to be earned, but maybe this is the first step toward it. I thought I was big and bad, but I ain't too big and bad to apologize. I think we can run the table this year. I know if we're united, we can win state. Forgive me, you guys? Anybody with me? Can we do this together?"

"Can you play?" Wax yelled out. "I need a quarterback who's gonna throw me the ball. When I run this thing, they aren't going to know what hit them. Dual threat."

I smiled, knowing that if Wax was cool, everyone else would follow our senior stud. "My arm's gonna be right. I'm ready. Lions, Lions ..."

"Lions, Lions, Lions," the team all started cheering with me.

After the hype, the guys started filing out of the locker room. I spoke to different players, apologizing to some, and giving others positive pointers. I knew there was a couple more guys I needed to rap to.

Landon was almost to his car, and I jogged over there to catch him. "Can I talk to you for a sec?"

"What's up, man?" Landon said in an uptight tone, confirming the air between us wasn't clear.

"I just owe you a bigger apology in addition to the one I gave the whole team. I would not have even been able to talk to them if you hadn't quieted them down and got them to stay."

Surprisingly, he said, "You called me out. I wasn't playing with true heart. I ain't mad at you for that."

"Yeah, but I didn't have to be so rough about it. You my boy."

Landon pointed to my shoulder. "I think you got what was coming to you when you got knocked on your tail the next play."

"You right, the whole ordeal definitely made me appreciate all I do have going on. I need you as my partna. I don't like us not hanging out. We cool?"

"Me and you straight. You need to work it out with him," Landon said, giving me five and then pointing over to Brenton. "You must not have heard what happened in school today."

"No, I've been trying to get this shoulder right, going to see the trainer in between classes. I am hoping I can play Friday night. What's up?"

"He likes your girl."

"I knew that. He has wanted Charli since nursery school."

Landon shook his head. "Oh, so you got jokes? You aren't gonna be laughing long."

"Why you say that? You think she likes him?"

"News flash, cuz. He kissed her today in the cafeteria. Everybody saw and was tweeting."

That info struck a cord in me that wasn't a nice sound. I looked over at Brenton, and he was frowning my way. He walked over to us.

I asked, "You need a ride home, B? Hoping we could talk while we rode."

Nonchalantly Brenton said, "Nah, I'm straight. Landon's got me."

Landon said, "Nah, nah, ride wit'cha cuz. Y'all need to talk."

"I don't think that's a good idea," Brenton said, waiting for Landon to open his passenger door. "You gonna take me home, Landon, or what?"

Landon shrugged his shoulder at me, like he tried to help. I nodded to let him know it was cool. Shoot, I didn't want to force my cousin to speak to me. Before I knew it, Landon unlocked the door for Brenton. They got in the car, and the two of them were gone.

"I know you mad. He wants your girl bad," Leo said, sneaking up behind me. "But maybe you don't care. Hottie Jackie telling everybody she with you now. I guess I need to give you some dap. You found a way to get you some, huh? So you can't be sweating Charli; she just tryna hold hands. That's right up Brenton's alley."

Leo laughed. I did not laugh. So much was happening, and I did not know how I felt about it all.

"Wow, Brenton is really going after Charli. Interesting."

Leo said, "You have always been a pretty boy, but you ain't player material."

"You right. I really don't need to be focused on no girl anyway. I'm trying to handle business on Friday nights. Plus, I've got some AP classes now that I gotta be on top of," I said. I bowed my head as I realized that I still cared about Charli. I wished I didn't.

"Look, man, I just came over here to tell you I'm happy you said what you said to the team. We need you. Don't go tripping again and go work things out with Brenton because he's the leader of the defense, and we don't need our two leaders at odds over a girl who you say you don't care about. But whatever, I do not believe that."

"I hear you, man. I'll talk to him," I said, knowing it was my responsibility to make amends. We slapped hands before Leo took off with some other players.

I looked over at my dad's car. He gave me a thumb-up, and it was just a little gesture, but it was one that meant a lot. He told me earlier that he was proud of me because I challenged my teammates. Letting them see I was vulnerable, he smiled approvingly, being proud of me for that too.

Driving, I thought of the love square I'd created with Brenton, Charli, and Jackie. What was I going to do with that? And why did love have to mess up a brother anyway?

It was the first game of the season. All I'd been working on for months was upon me. How you get out of the gate counts. If you want to stay on the top of the leader board, you got to produce early in the season.

Our band was rocking. Fans were filling the stands, and the cheerleaders looked so sweet, particularly Charli. I was trying to not let my mind think of her. However, since I found out my cousin placed his lips on hers, I was stressed about it. I wasn't mad at either of them. From what I heard though, she didn't pull back. I couldn't be mad at him for going there because he had always told me if I didn't behave, he was going to be there to take her.

The dance team was in the end zone performing a number. When they were done, Jackie headed over to me on the sidelines as I was getting some Gatorade. I had to stay hydrated so I wouldn't cramp up. Though it was a night game, it was still hot in Georgia. Since I was not one hundred percent sure that my shoulder was ready, I needed the rest of my system to be on point.

"I miss you, Blake," Jackie said, as her hand went up my jersey.

I heard her talking to me. I remembered the amazing night we shared. However, I could not stop my mind from looking across the fence and seeing adorable Charli Black.

Moving away she said, "Blake, are you even listening?"

I had not promised Jackie anything. No commitment was made. She was not my girl. We were just kicking it that one time. While it certainly was not my intent to hit it and go, I never looked back, never called her again, and never tried to take her out on a real date.

Peeking over at Charli, I wondered why I was tripping. I had no clue why I was stuck on something I passed up. I could not get my eyes off Charli.

Jackie said, "Are you listening?"

Quickly looking back at Jackie, I said, "Yes."

When my eyes roamed back over to where the cheerleaders stood, Charli was gone. I moved my attention from Jackie. I searched the track, and I found Charli upset with her girls all around consoling her. Did she want me too? Did she see Jackie's hands on me and get upset? I knew I needed to figure it out. Something inside of me made me forget about football—forget that in fifteen minutes I was going to have to suit up and play. I ignored the thought that if my dad saw me talking to a girl, he'd have my hide. None of that mattered because I saw a girl who I cared for in distress.

With Jackie I was preoccupied, and that told me I needed to speak to Charli right away.

I had to find out if I could rectify my mistake. I excused myself from Jackie and headed over to the girl I wanted back.

Her girls gave us privacy. Charli batted her eyes at me and smiled. I started apologizing. However, like I was with Jackie, I could tell Charli was half into what I was saying. I looked behind me and noticed the problem. Though Charli was standing before me listening to what I had to say, clearly her eyes and her heart were elsewhere. Brenton stood behind me, peering over in our direction.

That's when I knew I had a decision to make. Brenton had always been true about his feelings for Charli. I was always indecisive. It touched me that she came to me the second day of school saying she was sorry about my mom, and had she known, she would've made time to be there for me. But I had already moved on. It was not fair for me to keep leading her on.

Seeing she was torn, I kissed her cheek and whispered, "Go to Brenton."

She smiled at me in a way that made me feel real good about doing the right thing. When she went to my cousin, he did not seem too interested. However, I knew that was because he did not know what I had told her and probably did not want to deal with coming in second again.

When we were in the locker room, I went over to him. He rolled his eyes my way. Maybe he thought I was coming over to gloat. That was not the case. I pushed him in the back.

"Get off me, man," Brenton said, as he came to my face.

I pushed him again, but this time from the front. He pushed me back. Anger was written all over his face.

"That's what I'm talking about. Fight for something," I yelled.

"There's no need to fight," he said to me.

"Sometimes it's every reason to fight. I messed up. You got the girl," I said boldly.

"Whatever," Brenton said with our teammates surrounding us. "I can't deal with her being with me sometimes and then with you other times. It's just not what I wanna deal with."

I came closer and said, "Look, Charli's a special girl. I know that now. We both have interest, but the best man for her won. She wants and needs you."

He pushed me back and said, "And don't you forget it. I've always liked her, man. It's not about looks. It's not about sex. It's just about Charli. She's just—"

"I know, like I said, she's special. Take care of her, cuz," I said.

My dad called the team to the center of the locker room. "All right, guys. It's the first game of the season, show time. I want to apologize to y'all for being a little crazy at times this summer, but Blake and I have been going through something personal. Some of you may have heard, but I do want to confirm that my wife's been diagnosed with cancer. She had her first radiation treatment today, and she's remarkably strong. I didn't want her to come to this game. The doctor told her she needed to get her rest, but she said she wouldn't miss this for the world. Mrs. Strong has to cheer on the Lions, and if she can muster up the strength to sit in those stands to be here for you guys, then you find a way to play your hardest for her, for each other, and for yourselves. All hands in, 1 … 2 … 3 …"

And we all yelled, "Lions."

It was fourth quarter, and we were down by three points. I had the ball, and there were two minutes, three seconds left on the clock. We needed a TD to win.

In the huddle with my offense, I said, "It's been a tough night for the defense guys. We've been going back and forth, but we're in this thing. We can do this. Wax, I'm going to hand it off to you. Toss it back to me, and I'll throw it deep to the left corner."

"I don't know if I can catch it, man," Landon said, remembering the couple times he choked.

I placed my hand on his shoulder pad and said, "Look, dude, we gonna win this game."

"I had two corners sweating me all night," Landon said.

"So what? Shake them off, take them out, find a way to be open. You can do it," I encouraged.

"They gonna think I got the mail," Wax said also telling Landon to relax and just play. "I'm sitting on one hundred forty yards. We gonna fake 'em out."

When I said hike, it was on. I handed the ball off to Wax, faked like I kept it, and had defenders following me. But when they realized Wax had the ball and switched to defend him, he threw it back to me. He was able to do that because we had not crossed the line of scrimmage.

Landon was far down field. Knowing I had not thrown a deep ball all night, I was actually a little scared of my shoulder. However, just like I told Landon he could do it, I had to believe I could as well. I threw the pigskin up in the air, and it was caught by my boy for a sweet touchdown.

The crowd went wild. My dad was going nuts. He was about to get thrown out of the game for being all over the field. My team was pumped. We only hoped that we did not score too soon because there were still forty seconds left on the clock. Our kicker showed up, pinned it deep down, and I went up to Brenton to say a good word.

I said, "You got this."

"That's right, man. We had a tough one tonight, but you guys held it up for us. We won't let them score. Some things are worth fighting for."

He smiled, put on his helmet, and jogged onto the field. Sure enough, the clock wound down and we won.

At the after party, Jackie was standing alone. I knew I owed her some type of explanation. I went over to her and stood beside her.

I said, "Can we dance?

"You know I want more than a dance. I give myself to you, and you give me the cold shoulder," Jackie replied with attitude.

"I'm sorry," I said. I truly felt bad, but I didn't know what else to say.

"I want more than that," Jackie said. "You want Charli though, right?"

"That's over," I responded, knowing it was the truth.

Being intuitive, she said, "But that didn't answer my question."

"I don't know what more I can tell you. She was my girl for a long time. To be honest, I'm gonna have feelings for her, but you knew that already."

"I just thought with what we shared, she'd be history, ya know? I give you all I got, and that's not enough to erase her memory? I want your whole heart, Blake. Charli called me out in school, and she told me I get what I deserve. I did know y'all were involved. You're right. I can't just expect your feelings to just flip off like a switch. But I can't share you. I won't do that."

"Well, if you're willing to try and take it slow ... I got a lot on me right now, and you know that. My mom is sick. I've got to keep my grades up. I want you in my life; don't get me wrong but ..."

"As long as you're telling me you want to give us a try, then we'll make it work," she said, taking my hand.

When she put her hand around my neck and pulled my lips toward hers, I felt I was right where I was supposed to be. Jackie did get me excited. She did not want to compromise who she was. She still wanted to show herself off a little too much for my comfort level. As long as she knew I wasn't signing up to say we were boyfriend and girlfriend and all of that, then maybe we could figure this thing out. As long as both of us were having fun and nobody was getting hurt, then what was the problem?

Later on that evening my Mom and Dad were nestled in front of the TV. He was as happy as he could be. The ole ball coach had gotten a *W* in the win column. My mom was holding up. She looked good. Lola was over at a friend's place, so the house was quiet.

My mom said, "Give me a hug, son. Good game."

"Are you okay, Mom?" I said, needing a double check.

"Don't I look fine?" she joked.

"You know you didn't have to come to the game. You should have been getting some rest."

"I'm resting now, and I did have to come. I told you I'm going to be there. You're not going to get away that easily."

We both smiled. I loved that lady, and I was thankful she was happy. My mom had grace, even going through the drama of the past couple of weeks. If she was upbeat, then I would be too.

My dad said, "Why don't you go check on the kitchen table? Some mail came for you."

"Mail for me?" I asked, wondering if it was a school.

He eyed me, letting me know it was the kind of mail we both wanted. "Yeah."

I had headed over, and I knew it had to be something from the University of Florida. My dad made sure I got in his alma mater's system in the ninth grade. The way he was smiling, it had to be something from the Gators.

I was surprised when I saw Notre Dame's letterhead. I looked at my father, and he was standing tall and proud. I tore open the letter. It read:

Congratulations Blake,

The University of Notre Dame is pleased to inform you that we will be recruiting you. We believe you have talent, character, and heart. We feel Notre Dame will be the perfect institution for you. We will be following you all season long and would love to have you come up for an official visit. Call if you have any questions.

Sincerely,

The Head Coach

"Dad, Dad!" I yelled.

"I know, son. They called the school wanting your transcript. The Fighting Irish are serious about recruiting you. I know you do not want to be a Gator. Your loss though, cuz," my dad teased. "I'm proud of you, son. You're a playmaker with options."

"But I don't want you to go that far," my mom said.

"If the Irish call, Mom, I'm going to have to go."

"Be proud of yourself," my father said.

It had been a rough summer and a rocky start to the school year, but things had smoothed out. I learned you can't take women for granted. If you snooze on a good relationship, aren't able to deal with your problems, push your teammates too far, and get too cocky, you'll find yourself isolated. However, if you lead, care about all, own up to your own mistakes, do better next time, have hope and faith, then things do work out. The events of life can have happy endings if you stay calm. During a two-minute drive, you not only have to be a playmaker, but a way maker.

STEPHANIE PERRY MOORE is the author of many YA inspirational fiction titles, including the *Payton Skky* series, the *Laurel Shadrach* series, the *Perry Skky Jr.* series, the *Yasmin Peace* series, the *Faith Thomas Novelzine* series, the *Carmen Browne* series, the *Morgan Love* series, and the *Beta Gamma Pi* series. Mrs. Moore speaks with young people across the country, encouraging them to achieve every attainable dream. She currently lives in the greater Atlanta area with her husband, Derrick, and their three children. Visit her website at www.stephanieperrymoore.com.

DERRICK MOORE is a former NFL running back and currently the developmental coach for the Georiga Institute of Technology. He is also the author of *The Great Adventure* and *It's Possible: Turning Your Dreams into Reality*. Mr. Moore is a motivational speaker and shares with audiences everywhere how to climb the mountain in their lives and not stop until they have reached the top. He and his wife, Stephanie, have co-authored the *Alec London* series. Visit his website at www.derrickmoorespeaking.com.

WANT A DIFFERENT
point of view?

JUST *flip* THE BOOK!

The Lockwood High che... ...as it all—sass, looks, and all the right moves. But everything isn't always as perfect as it seems. Because where there's cheer, there's drama. And then there's the ballers—hot, tough, and on point. But what's going to win out—life's pressures or their NFL dreams?

CHARLI
CHEER
Drama

Savvy Charli Black seems to have the perfect life ...
but perfect isn't always what it seems.

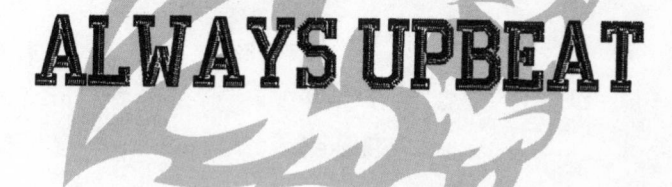

ALWAYS UPBEAT

Stephanie Perry Moore

SADDLEBACK
EDUCATIONAL PUBLISHING

CHEER DRAMA

Always Upbeat

Keep Jumping

Yell Out

Settle Down

Shake It

SADDLEBACK
EDUCATIONAL PUBLISHING
www.sdlback.com

ISBN-13: 978-1-61651-884-4
ISBN-10: 1-61651-884-7
eBook: 978-1-61247-618-6

Printed in Guangzhou, China
0212/CA21200344

16 15 14 13 12   1 2 3 4 5

To Tammy Garnes

We know drama, don't we lady?
I just wanted to say that your belief in my work
touched my soul. Though we're still climbing
toward our goals, know that I wish you the best.
May every reader be as strong of a leader as you.

Stay upbeat and go get your dreams …
I love you!

ACKNOWLEDGEMENTS

It is hard to stay positive when things don't seem to be going your way. You don't have to tell me. All I've wanted to do since I was in the 7th grade was write for film and television. I'm many years from those days, and I still have not had my heart's desire realized. I am so close, and I hope it works out as I am daily trying to making my dream a reality. However, I get frustrated when doors don't open. When people who can, don't help. When it seems like it will never work out. Shoot, life gets tough.

Nonetheless, I have learned to be thankful for what I have. In the midst of writing this first book in the Cheer Drama series, I was blessed to get another deal for another series. I also received a contract to be the co-editor of a new bible. Even though I don't have a deal yet, one of my scripts is in the hands of a major studio. I know those great opportunities only came my way because I stayed upbeat. Point to you, reader, don't waste time whining. Forge ahead and before you know it, all will work out the way it is supposed to.

Acknowledgements

Here is a big thank you to the ones who are helping me stay pumped up and productive.

For my parents, Dr. Franklin and Shirley Perry Sr., thanks for your support that is always there. For my publisher, especially Tim McHugh, thanks for your enthusiasm for my work and for the opportunity to be a part of your great team.

For my extended family: brother, Dennis Perry, godmother, Majorie Kimbrough, mother-in-law, Ann Redding, brother-in-Christ, Jay Spencer, and goddaughter, Danielle Lynn, thanks for cheering me on.

For my assistants: Alyxandra Pinkston and Joy Spencer, thanks ladies for being fired up with me to get this novel done.

For my friends who are dear to my heart: Lakeba Williams, Leslie Perry, Sarah Lundy, Jenell Clark, Nicole Smith, Jackie Dixon, Torian Colon, Loni Perriman, Kim Forest, Vickie Davis, Kim Monroe, Jamell Meeks, Michele Jenkins, Lois Barney, Veronica Evans, Laurie Weaver, Taiwanna Brown-Bolds, Matosha Glover, Yolanda Rodgers-Howsie, Dayna Fleming, Denise Gilmore, and Deborah Bradley, thanks for being fired up to be my girls.

For my teens: Dustyn, Sydni, and Sheldyn, thanks for giving me a reason to root hard and love unconditionally.

For my husband, Derrick, thanks for always being in my corner and helping me do this.

For my new readers, thanks for trying this book and reading.

And for my Savior, thanks for ordering my steps in the direction that led me to opportunity where I can partner with Saddleback and help others obtain a passion for reading.

CHAPTER 1

Picked Me

You are so beautiful, Charli," my boyfriend, Blake, whispered in my ear. He was six foot one and two hundred pounds of handsome. We sat at the food court in the happening Southlake Mall, enjoying each other.

I blushed. He had my heart. Blake Strong was every girl's dream. He was gorgeous and smart. Plus he was the starting quarterback at our upscale and predominantly African American Lockwood High School near the Atlanta airport. Though his dad was the football coach and a tough PE teacher, who scared us all, Blake was the complete opposite: just a teddy bear, and he was mine.

My life was fantastic. People said I was spoiled. I was an only child. My father was a state judge. So a princess's lifestyle was pretty much my story.

While my mom was busy with clubs, luncheons, and charities, I knew she loved me. She was there for everything I needed. There was not a ballet recital, tennis match, or cheerleading competition that she ever missed. My father and I were truly blessed to have her attend to all our needs.

Though I probably wouldn't win *America's Next Top Model*, when I walked in the room, dudes were eyeing me. At five foot six, size 8 shoe, and size 4 clothes ... okay, really a size 6, my curves were in the right places. I didn't have any eating disorder issues. But keeping it real, I was not going to put anything too fattening in my mouth. Like most teen girls, I was conscious of my appearance. So when Blake told me I was beautiful, he had me melting.

"Nobody's at my house, Charli Black," Blake said, laughing. "You know your name should be Charlie Brown."

I just hit him, even though I get that all the

time. His smile was perfect, and his hair was naturally wavy like mine. If my mother knew my thoughts, she'd kill me, but we'd have some pur-tee babies. Course we would actually have to do something for that to be an issue, and my mom would be pleased to know my legs had never been opened in that manner.

As he leaned in and kissed me on my neck, Blake continued, "Football camp starts tomorrow. You'll be going to cheerleading practice every day the next few weeks. Today is our day, babe. Let's really be together."

He took my hand and motioned for us to leave. While I wanted to make him happy, I was not ready to commit myself. I knew a couple of my girls were out there having fun. And though I knew I loved Blake, something inside of me was saying to hold off giving it all up. I could not let him push me, so I tugged away.

"Oh, so it's like that?" he asked, getting a little frustrated that I told him no in a subtle way.

"Soon. Okay, baby?" I asked, sliding my hand up his chest.

"Don't play. Don't get me all excited and then tell me no. I'm going to get some ice cream."

Blake got up and shoved his chair hard under the table.

When he walked away, I could not stop keeping my eyes centered below his waist. The brown, luscious brother was fine. What was I thinking? What was I doing? What was I risking?

I needed to talk to my girls. Problem was, they were probably all together. And if one knew my business, they all would know. I had four great girlfriends. We had challenges, and we were not alike. But we all agreed how exciting it was to be the juniors on the cheerleading squad.

Everybody called me the most confident, but they did not know I really had my own issues. My mom taught me how to walk with my head up high, however, I always felt like I was not measuring up to her high standards.

Hallie was the loudest out of our group. You always knew when she was coming. She was not the best cheerleader. Honestly, we did not know if she was going to make the team. She had been trying for the past two years. The third time was the charm.

There were twins Ella and Eva. Though they looked identical, they were nothing alike.

Ella was a sweetheart, and Eva was sneaky, salty, and snappy. When you put the two of them together, it was like the perfect glass of Kool-Aid, but split them up and you got too much sugar or too much salt.

And Randal was my girl. She was so shy, but the better part of us all in my opinion. She did not give herself enough credit. She was always down on herself, and I did not like that. I loved that she had my same values of wanting to wait for sex. That was her goal, too, though it was easier for her because she did not have a man.

It was not so easy trying to stay pure when you had somebody stand in front of you looking all good, nibbling on your ear, and putting his hands everywhere they did not belong. I needed encouragement to stay strong so I would not go find Blake, jump in his car, and let him have his way with me.

Answering Randal's phone, Eva said, "Wassup, Charli? Girl, thought you'd be too busy with Blake to call."

With little enthusiasm, I replied, "Hey, Eva."

"Don't sound like you ain't excited to talk to me. Whatever ... Here, Randal. It's your girl.

She's acting funky," Eva said. "I don't have time for the attitude."

"I don't have an attitude," I said, hoping Eva would hear me before Randal got the cell.

In a kinder tone, Randal said, "Hey, Charli. How are you?"

"Hanging," I replied, taking a deep breath. "What are y'all doing?"

"They're over, and we are trying to teach Hallie some cheers," Randal answered.

Snatching the phone, Hallie said, "I don't want to look like a complete idiot at practice tomorrow, not knowing nothing. I wish you were here."

"It's not knowing anything," I thought to myself, not nothing. However, I knew I couldn't correct Hallie, because I'd never hear the end of it. In our group, Ella was the smartest one of us, although I wasn't far behind in the scholastic department. But the other three, for the life of me, stressed me out with the ghetto talk all the time.

"But you're with Blake," Hallie said loudly into the phone.

Hearing them laugh and tease me, I said, "Well, y'all are busy. I'll let you go."

I could sense Randal wrestling Hallie for the phone. "I've always got time to talk to you. Wassup?" Randal asked.

"Nothing, it's fine. Go practice."

Eva said, "Charli, I just pushed her intercom button. You're on speaker. Spill it, dang."

Feeling forced, I said, "Hey, you guys."

"Hey, Charli. Miss you, girl," Ella said in a warmer tone, making me feel loved.

"I miss you too," I said, sending smooches through the phone. "How was New York?"

"Oh, so you can talk to my sister, but you ain't wanna talk to me?" Eva said with more attitude than a girl being upset with her hair-dresser for giving her a tore-up weave job.

Getting passionate because she was so wrong, I said, "Girl, don't even trip. You know I missed you too. You were at your grandma's for a whole month. I was about to get on a plane and fly to New York myself to hang out with you guys. Tell them, Hallie. We looked up tickets."

Hallie had my back. "Yeah, we did."

"We're straight. But for real, Charli. You're with your man. Why are you calling us?" Eva asked. "Where is he?"

I looked over at the Dairy Queen. He said he was getting some ice cream, but I didn't see him standing there. My eyes started searching frantically. Where was my fine beau? My eyes widened when I spotted him laughing with some chick I recognized from our school.

"Who is that he's talking to? Why does she have her hand all over him like that? He's smiling at her!"

There were lots of oohs and ahhs going on in the background. Then I realized I was telling my friends *way* too much. All four of them started speaking to me at once, and it wasn't that I was ever dishonest with them, but I did not want them to know there was trouble in paradise. I was supposed to be the one who had it together.

Why was my boyfriend standing over there talking to some fast-looking girl? If her skirt was any higher, she would not have one on. Her shirt might as well have been a bikini top that was two sizes too small because everything was showing.

Truly upset and keeping it real, I yelled, "Oh heck nah. Y'all, I got to go."

I had done too much work with Blake since freshman year—to get him to be the right boyfriend—for some girl to come along junior year and think she was going to take him. It was not going to happen.

"Okay, you need to handle that," Eva said. "Because when you let go of the dog leash, they run all over the place. Chain him back up, girl."

"For real, or put him on the phone; I'll give him an earful. He knows he wrong for that, being all up in the mall flirting with some other girl," Hallie said.

I hung up the phone and went over to the two of them. I wasn't imagining everything I had seen from a distance. The two of them were clearly into each other. And as much as I wanted to tell myself it was all her, Blake was acting like he didn't have a girlfriend.

"Ugh," I said, stepping between them. "Excuse me."

Caught, my idiot boyfriend said, "Oh, oh, Charli. You know Jackie from school, right?"

"No, I've seen her, but I don't know her. You don't need to know her either." I rolled my eyes at both of them.

"I have enough girlfriends, Blake," Jackie said, licking her fingertip suggestively. "I want something else," she said.

I snatched him away really fast. "Okay, so what's *that* all about?"

"Nothing, you didn't have to be all rude to the girl."

"Whatever! She was rude to me. I know you're not going to defend her. Blake, I'm with you at the mall, and this is how you act when you step away. How do you act when I'm not even around? Am I really the girl you want or what?"

Then I walked away. He came up behind me, put his arms around my waist, and said, "You know you the girl for me. You ain't got to worry 'bout nobody."

I took a deep breath and felt better after he reassured me. Thankfully we were good, but I knew I was going to have to do whatever was needed for things to stay that way.

I had been rambling on and on about Blake when I heard Eva say, "Like she thinks we're supposed to sit here and listen to her talk about Blake all day."

I said, "Sorry, Eva. I didn't know coming to my girls for advice was selfish."

"Ignore her," Ella said, as she stroked my shoulder.

"I'm just saying," Eva replied. "We already know he was checking out someone else, and that person was checking out him. But who was it? You said you thought you knew her. Does she go to our school? We can't help you understand any of it and break it down unless you divulge all."

Frustrated, I uttered, "A girl named Jackie. I think she's on the dance team."

"Jackie ... ooh Jackie?" Randal said, using her hands to make curvy body motions.

Reluctantly, I nodded. Hallie looked at Ella. Ella looked at Randal. Randal looked at Eva. And Eva looked at me like they all knew something I did not.

Eva just busted out and said, "Okay, words out ... she really likes Blake. Just so you know, we were hoping it was anybody but her."

"What? What do you mean?" I asked in a desperate tone.

"Well, last year she was in my language arts class and so was Blake and ..."

"And what? You never told me anything about that," I said

Nonchalantly, Eva said, "I didn't think there was anything to tell. Guys are going to be guys."

I stepped to Eva and said, "What do you mean? He's my boyfriend, Eva! Darn, I thought you had my back."

"I do, but I can't tell your man what to do. If he's looking at somebody else, and I brought that to you, you would just dismiss it. We been here and done that already, so don't play. We already got into it in ninth grade about Blake. I tried to tell you then he was a player, and you didn't listen. So, I mean, you know, don't blame me." Eva gave me a cold, coy grin.

Opening up her bedroom door and peeking out, Randal said, "You guys, calm down before my mom comes in here and wonders what in the world is going on."

"Y'all need to get Charli up out of my face," Eva said.

I thought back to ninth grade. She and I really did go at it about Blake. Every day she was telling me about this girl and that girl. When I talked to him about it, he told me what was really

up. Apparently, Eva tried to get with him, and then he chose me over her. She was salty. It had been two years since all that drama, and I really thought we were past that, but maybe deep down a part of her didn't care if Blake ditched me. My friendship with Eva was sometimey, and I just needed her to care.

"So what did Blake say when you confronted him for talking to jack-butt Jackie?" Hallie asked. Randal and Ella laughed at her shrewd choice of nickname.

"He told me it was nothing. He told me he didn't like her, and that I didn't have to worry."

Ella put her arm around me. "So what are you tripping about?" she asked.

"You're beautiful. He's crazy about you. He's probably the most popular guy in school, even as a junior. But still, everybody knows he's yours," Randal said.

"Yeah, don't let him see you sweat," Hallie said, smiling. I knew she wanted something, so I let her ramble on. "So now that you're feeling better, Miss Best Cheerleader in America, can you please help teach me some moves? All them three been doing is eating Randal's mom's food."

Eva added, "Whatever. We can't help that she's a caterer and kept asking us to sample."

Shaking my head to try and get it together, I said, "You're right. I need to get my mind off of Blake. Let's go. Let's do the cheer. Which one do you want to learn?"

Hallie jumped up and down. "Teach me 'Who Dat?'"

"You ain't said nothing but a word," Eva said. Then she came over and stood beside me, and the two of us threw down—cheering squashed the drama.

Grooving, I chanted, "Who dat? Who dat? Who dat think they bad? Who dat? Who dat? We're going to kick them in their … Clap, clap, clap. Step up, step back, shake, shake, shake. Arms up, arms down, your fist all around and come by your waist. Clap, clap, clap. Kick ball change, step up—"

"Wait, wait, wait, I can't," Hallie said, cutting us off. "That's too hard."

Eva gave Hallie a stern glare. "Girl, you got to be able to step in and pick it up. We ain't even doing the precision cheers. This is just *feel the beat* with a little soul. Come on now."

Randal and Ella joined us, and then we started making up new steps. Eva followed me. I followed her. The four of us were jamming, but Hallie looked lost. Upset, she ran out of Randal's room.

"I got her, y'all," I said to my friends.

Hallie went into the bathroom. I did not like her to be down on herself. She could get this.

I knocked on the door. "It's me, Charli. Let me in, please."

"No, just go."

"Hallie, come on, girl. Let me in. Please, girl."

Finally, when she opened up the door, I said, "Talk to me. Why are you crying? You're on the squad. You'll get all this."

"I need to have it now. I don't want to be the laughing stock of the varsity cheerleading team. Word's out. The only reason I made it was because they needed to have an even number, and they didn't want to give it to another sophomore."

I said, "People are always making up stuff. I never heard that."

"Yes, you did, Charli. You just didn't want to hurt my feelings."

"Look," I said, taking both of Hallie's hands. "I'll work with you day and night to make sure you learn all the cheers. I'll stand beside you in practice. You have rhythm, and you have the biggest mouth out of anyone I know. Take that the right way. For cheerleading, it's perfect. You just gotta project, be confident, get excited, and do the moves."

"Yeah, but it's like when you stand in front of me and teach me … I get all the moves twisted and backwards, and I can't do it."

"Well, that's all you had to say. If that's more confusing, then I'm going to stand right beside you. Watch me. Who dat? And we step up. Who dat? And we step back. Who dat think they bad? And we shake our hips. Who dat? We put our arms down. Who dat? We put our arms up. Then we do the kick ball change as much as we can because we're in the bathroom," I said, as Hallie laughed. "We're going to kick them in their … turn and give three claps. That's all it is, and you just do it faster. Let's go."

After about twenty times, Hallie had it. She gave me the biggest hug ever. She screamed. Randal's mom came running down the hall.

The blue-eyed-blonde Mrs. Raines said, "Is everything okay?"

Randal came running into the bathroom, "I told y'all not to jump and all that stuff when she's baking. She gets freaked out," Randal sighed. Poking her head out the door, she declared "Everything's fine, Mom. We're going back to my room."

Randal shooed her mom down the hall. "You girls be careful," Mrs. Raines said, looking glum.

Bragging on my girl, I said, "Do it, Hallie. Show them the cheer."

"We know she doesn't have it," Eva said under her breath.

"Eva, goodness gracious, girl. Dang. Why do you have to be so negative?" I finally just said to her because I was tired of her always having something smart to say.

Classic Eva vented, "'Cause Hallie wants to be a cheerleader so bad, but then she starts crying like a kindergartner when she can't get the moves. We're on varsity. Honestly, maybe she should have made JV, if anything. All of us were wondering why she made the team. Let's just be honest."

Tears started welling up in Hallie's eyes. I just looked at Eva and rolled mine. Eva needed to learn to hush up sometimes.

Believing in my girl, I said, "Don't even let her affect you. She doesn't speak for all of us. Do the doggone cheer. You have it. Do it!"

I started doing it when Hallie wouldn't. And just doing what I do, I didn't even realize Hallie joined in, and we were in unison throwing down.

Eva said, "My bad, girl. That's it. And you know I was teasing. I needed to motivate you to do the doggone thing."

I smiled at Eva like, *You got me again, dang it*. I couldn't figure her out, but under all the layers there was love in Eva's heart. We hugged.

"You know we pick captains tomorrow," Ella said. "And, Charli. It needs to be you."

"Like they're going to elect me captain. It's just five of us juniors, five sophomores, and ten seniors on this squad. No way they're going to choose me."

"Well, you're the best. You got what it takes. We're going to find a way to get you to be captain," Eva said, surprising me because she cared.

"You're the best, and you got a way of pulling out the best in everybody. When the five of us put our minds to it, we can do it," Hallie said.

"I just love y'all," I said to them. "Drama and all."

Eva winked, and then I thought, "Me, *captain*? ... That would be amazing."

"Charli, do you need me to take you to practice, honey. I'm going that way," my mother said, as I was about to head out the door.

However, Blake was honking. I could not keep him waiting. I certainly was not going to tell him to leave so she could take me.

"No, Mom. Blake's here. Thanks though. Smooches!" I said, rushing out the door.

"Be—"

Before she could say careful, I was gone. I was not trying to be rude, but she was getting on my nerves. She had been telling my dad that I did not need to drive. She wanted me to wait until my senior year. He wanted to buy me a car. I needed a car, and I deserved one. If she was going to stand in the way of that, then I was going to hate on her a little bit.

"Hey, baby!" I said when I got into his car.

With a slight 'tude, Blake said, "What took you so long? You know my dad is going to kill me if I'm late for practice."

"I'm sorry," I purred, still wanting a kiss.

Then his cell phone started vibrating. As soon as I grabbed it, he snatched it out of my hands.

"You know you don't read my messages. Wassup with that?"

"What? You trying to hide something from me?" I asked, truly unsure.

Frowning, he sped down the street. "Why you always do that?"

"What?" I put on my seat belt.

"Starting beef with me. Shoot, I came all the way over here to pick you up so I could see my girl before practice. You know it's going to be hot as heck out there. My dad's going to run and work us hard. I'm just trying to chill and relax. You stressin' a brother and stuff."

At that point I looked out the window. Blake and I were growing apart, and there was nothing I could really do about it. As much as I wanted to make him happy, to say the right things so that our relationship stayed good, things kept

messing up. I really didn't know where we were headed. Particularly when his phone vibrated again, and he didn't answer it.

"We're probably going to have an extra long practice today, so don't wait around. Get a ride from one of your girls or something," he said when we got to the school parking lot.

"No problem," I said, as I got out of the car.

We were the Lockwood Lions. The purple and gold. This was supposed to be our year. Blake, the quarterback of the football team, doing his thing, running the ball in, throwing the long bombs that get caught for touchdowns, just being a stud. And me, his girl on the sideline, wowing the crowd with my moves, and making all girls in the stands wish they were in my shoes. But something wasn't right. And when the senior cheerleaders and their pack waved at my man and didn't even speak to me, and he got all goo-gooed like he was a baby, I knew there was trouble in paradise.

When some football players rolled up beside him, he tried to act like we were all cool.

"What, you not going to give me no love, no kiss, no smooch? Wassup, Charli?"

Trying to keep him whichever way I could, I went over to him and obliged his request. A few of the players gave him dap. He jogged off without even looking back at me. So caught up in being the man, he didn't even realize he was breaking my heart.

But then his cousin Brenton, a real sweetheart and way more laid back than show-off Blake, said, "Cheer up, Charli."

"I'm cool, Brenton. I'm not down."

"No smile on that cute face of yours. Something's up."

"No flirting with your cousin's girlfriend," I said.

"Maybe my cousin's girlfriend should want a real man versus a little boy who craves attention. But who am I to give advice, right? See you later."

My girls came out of nowhere. They were jammed in Hallie's ride, which was on its last legs but still kicking. "Ugh, did we just hear what we thought we heard?" Hallie said.

"Somebody likes you," Randal said.

"Nah, he was just being nice," I replied.

Coach Woods was standing by the door. "You girls better get in here. I know you're new to my

varsity squad, but I *will* make you run when you're late. I don't have time for prima donnas. Let's go. Let's go. Let's go."

"Dang, I didn't know we were joining the army," Eva said.

"Yeah, consider this boot camp," Coach Woods said, hearing her.

The rest of us just laughed. Coach Woods was really cute, fly actually. She made the boys' heads turn, and she was in her thirties or something. I know compared to my mom that wasn't old, but to us it was, and she was still holding it down. I hoped when I got older I would look like her. But she wasn't just one of them cute, ditsy ladies. Nah, she was smart— unlike our coach from last year who Eva walked all over. Eva made up stupid stories when she was late or missed practice, saying she was with this guy and that guy, and coach just believed whatever she said ... gullible. But it didn't look like Eva was going to get away with that stuff this year.

"Look who decided to join us," Whitney Alexander, the baddest girl in our school, said to us when we walked in.

Word was she was so bad when she was a freshman that she had all the senior girls hating her because she was holding down their men. She was also up for valedictorian, which was impressive to me. Anybody could look cute—perm, weave, wearing a flattering color, padded bra, stylish clothes, makeup, and the right shoes—and anybody's head could turn, but not everybody could be a scholar. However, there was one characteristic Whitney had that I detested, disliked, and couldn't stand. She was a snob, and she prided herself on it.

"Like you own this squad," Eva said, trying her.

"For real," Hallie said even louder.

"It must not be true because if I owned it, you wouldn't be on it with your lack of skills," Whitney said to Hallie.

"All right, girls, calm down. I don't want to hear all that," Coach Woods said immediately, spotting the mounting drama. "All you guys sit down right now."

The sophomores sat with each other. Whitney had a select group of seniors with her, and some other seniors were clustered together. And

of course me and my girls were seated beside each other.

"I'm not having this cliquish squad," Coach Woods said. "Yeah, it's great and fun, and we cheer for the Lions on Friday night. But our ultimate goal is to be state cheerleading champs for Class 5A. Everybody on this squad except one has a back handspring. Most of you guys have higher skills than that, but whatever area you're weak in, you need to work on it," she continued. "You're on the squad because I knew you could do it. Do not slack up on me, and do not give each other drama! We must be a team, and every team needs leadership. Right now we're going to vote for captain, so at this time I want to take nominations."

Whitney jumped up. "I nominate myself, Whitney Tia Alexander."

Coach looked unimpressed. "Is there anybody else?"

No one said a word. I wanted it, but I didn't feel like nominating myself. Because I thought I could do it, didn't mean I really could. This was going to be my first year on the varsity squad. Although I have been a competition cheerleader

since I was three, volunteered to teach cheer-leading to little girls, and I had the highest tumbling, best jumps, and tightest positioning out of anybody on the squad, it did not mean that I should actually have the captain's job. It was only my first year on the varsity squad, after all.

Eva, being true to her word, raised her hand, and said, "Coach, I nominate Charli Black."

All heads turned quickly. Amazingly, one set of seniors started smiling and whispering to each other. The sophomores got super quiet and wide-eyed.

Whitney just burst out and said, "I know y'all are not going to vote for her. I'm the one with experience. I'm the one with respect ..."

And some of the other senior girls started coughing. Hallie hit me on the leg. I knew she was thinking that maybe I had a shot at this thing. The body language in the gym told me that politics were working in my favor.

"I'm just saying that I need to be the cap-tain. I can get you girls in shape. I know how to make you all that—like me. Charli probably doesn't even want the job. I'm your captain, right here."

Coach Woods looked over at me and said, "Charli, do you accept the nomination?"

I looked around. Ella nodded. Randal silently clapped. Hallie was silently mouthing "Yes, yes, yes," and Eva pushed me.

I said, "Yes, ma'am."

"Do you have anything to say?" Coach asked.

"I love cheerleading. I love our school. I'd give you guys all I have. I could help make up routines that I believe would be competitive at state. If given the chance, I won't let you down."

"Well, all right. Let's get to voting."

Thirty minutes later, Coach announced this year's varsity cheerleading captain was Charli Black. All four of my girls screamed around me. I was elated. The squad picked me.

CHAPTER 2
Cloud Nine

We gotta go celebrate! My treat," I screamed to my girls after practice was over. I was just announced as the new captain.

"You ain't said nothing but a word," Eva yelled out, as she gave me a high-five. "And we ain't going to no McDonald's either. I want IHOP."

"Like there's any difference," her sister, Ella, said.

Eva jerked her neck. "Instead of her breaking out twenty dollars, she'll be bringing out forty. There's a big difference."

Hallie yelled, "Pancakes for dinner, baby. Let's go."

Whitney was sitting over to the side, rocking back and forth, as if she was in a trance. "I'll be right there, you guys," I said.

"What do you want? Please go. You won, okay?" Whitney whined, as she saw me coming. "Like you're gonna know how to handle all the seniors."

Trying, I said, "I could use your help."

"But you're not going to be getting it. The squad spoke, and they chose who they wanted." Whitney sulked. "And they'll get what they get. Sooner or later, they'll realize they made the wrong decision. You might have had more training than the rest of us. Yeah, I saw your fine skills. I know you can do fulls, aerials, and your jumps are immaculate. But do you have what it takes to be a leader? I don't think so."

I started to say, "Do *you* have what it takes to be a leader? The vote says you don't." But I didn't need to hurt her with needless jabs like she was doing to me.

Instead I said, "You will like my style and—"

But she did not let me finish. She got up and stormed away. Coach Woods came up behind me and understood that I was disappointed in

Whitney's reaction. Honestly, I did want all of us to get along. I could only imagine when opponents speak after a presidential election, the loser is not happy. We were in high school. No one was going to the White House. This was about trying to win a state cheerleading title, and the right person needed to be in the job for that to happen. I firmly believed that was me.

I looked at Coach Woods and said, "I am gonna try to work with her."

"I know you'll be great. Whitney doesn't realize that though. She is good but her attitude is not. She got in her own way. You stay grounded. I've been around long enough to see power do crazy things to ladies."

"Yes, ma'am." I nodded, knowing I would never be difficult like Whitney.

Outside the gym, Ella walked over and said, "Don't sweat Whitney."

Randal came up to my other side and said, "You know she's just upset that she didn't win."

"But our girl did. Let's go celebrate!" Hallie said.

"That's out now. She's not celebrating with us." Eva had her lips stuck way out.

"Yes, we are. What are you talking about?" I said to her, not wanting her to spoil my moment.

Whitney had already tried to deflate my excitement. I didn't want anything else to pull me down. However, I saw Blake running up to me, smiling like he was into me—like he should be. My heart skipped two beats, and I forgot about everything else.

"I heard the news. My baby's the captain. Gimme some love." He leaned in and kissed me, and he wasn't letting go.

His personal display of affection was a little overboard. I knew cheerleaders, band members, football players, and who knew who else were watching. He would not let me pull away.

Flinching and frowning, I said, "People are around us."

As Blake's hand caressed my back, he whispered in my ear. "Then let's go somewhere alone. I wanna celebrate with you, baby. I'm the captain and you're the captain."

"Like I said, she is not going out with us anymore," Eva declared, working her neck and her hips in irritating positions.

As much as I wanted to be with Blake, Eva

had a right to be ticked. I said I was going out with my girls, and I couldn't just ditch them. But my man wasn't letting up, and he hadn't been into me like this in so long. I was caught between wanting to do two things, which was impossible.

Remembering he had plans, I said, "I thought you couldn't drive me after school?"

"My dad let us out early. What's the matter? You gonna hang with them or me?" Blake asked, pointing to my waiting girls. "You always say I'm putting you second, and now what's up with this?"

"What's up with this anyway, Blake? You act like you're all into my girl when you—" Eva mouthed off before Randal and Ella pulled her back.

"Whatever, Eva. You wish you could get with this," Blake said to her, not wanting to be called out.

"Blake?" I grunted, unhappy he was talking about my friend.

I certainly didn't want my boyfriend and one of my best friends going at it. Blake had to chill. Eva needed to let me handle this. Though

I was torn, I knew if it was one of them, they'd tend to their man, so I had to do the same.

"Just go to the car." I pushed him. "I'll be there in a second."

I turned to my girls. They all looked at me like I had truly let them down. My insides were hurting.

Saying the only thing I could think of given the situation, I explained, "Y'all know I'm nervous about Blake. You guys even said this other girl's after him. I need to put in some time. I didn't even know he was gonna want to hang out with me, or I wouldn't have said let's do something. But take the money. Go eat and don't be mad at me."

"We don't want your money," Randal said.

"Speak for yourself," Eva said, before she snatched the forty dollars out of my hand, and they left.

Minutes later, we were in Blake's car. "So you're captain, huh?" Blake asked. The tension was subsiding.

I didn't know where he was driving me, but he sure looked good doing it. His muscles were bulging from his chest. He didn't have a stench

from practice because he had showered. My man looked and smelled good enough to gobble up.

"Where are we?" I asked. We were heading into a neighborhood hit by the foreclosure crisis. There were homes that were partially built. Down in the cul-de-sac, Blake and I were isolated. He parked the car and reached over and reclined my seat. Before I knew it, we both shared my seat and the passion intensified. Our hands were roaming; our bodies were moving. We were in sync. Our shirts were off but when Blake took his hand down too low, I stopped it.

"Please, Charli. Not now. Let me give you the best celebration present. Captain to captain, I'ma show you how it's done. You're my girl. I want you. I want us. Give me what I need."

He kissed me again, and I did not want to stop him. I did not want to lose him. I did not want him to be mad, but the voice inside of me knew that I was not ready. I did not care what the consequences of saying no were. That was my freaking final answer, and he had to deal with it. Then I realized the upset look on his face meant I might lose him, and I could not hold back the emotion.

I started crying uncontrollably. "I'm sorry, Blake. I'm sorry. I thought I was ready, but I'm not. Don't leave me, please. I love you."

Absolutely surprising me, he looked over and wiped my eyes. He leaned in gently and kissed my forehead. He lifted my chin to his face.

My caring beau said, "I'm sorry for pushing you. I love you too, and I want this to be right for the both of us. It's okay."

"Really?" I asked, feeling so grateful he cared enough to wait.

He nodded. When I was in his embrace, I felt so secure. I felt so safe, so special, and so loved.

When Blake dropped me off at home, chaos awaited me. Both of my parents were yelling at each other at the top of their voices. I wanted the drama to end.

"Charlene, knowing where that child is, is your responsibility. She could be with anybody, anywhere. You're here all day. I don't understand why you don't know where she is. You got one job—taking care of this house. You can't even do that," my father yelled.

My mom lashed back at him. "You must think I'm stupid. All the after-hours meetings and stuff you been going to … right! If you care so much about your home and this family, where are you, Roger, most nights? You're not on the bench at seven in the evening. You know the importance of telling the truth. So what is *really* going on?"

What was my mom trying to say? I had been so into my own world, hanging out with my friends, being with my boyfriend, and practicing my cheer moves, that the last thing I thought about was my home. My parents' marriage really seemed to be in trouble. Before they said something they couldn't take back, I stepped into the room.

"Is everything okay?" I asked timidly, knowing it was not okay but hoping they'd stop saying hateful things to each other if they saw me.

"Ask your mother," my dad snarled, storming out of the kitchen.

"Charli, don't stand there looking at me like you're all disappointed. You're a big girl now. Adults argue," my mom said. She went over to the sink and leaned in as if she was trying to

collect herself. "And where were you, Charli? Don't even think about lying to me, saying you were with your friends. I talked to Hallie, and you were not riding with her. Your dad and I were worried sick. I called you, and you didn't answer your phone."

"My cell is dead, Mom."

"Well, you need to start taking the charger with you. You knew you didn't tell me where you were going after practice. That's absolutely irresponsible. I didn't know if you were at the school waiting for me to come and pick you up or what. So I went over there, and Coach said you were long gone."

Thinking back to practice, I asked, "Did she tell you the good news?"

"Yes, I know you're the captain. Under normal circumstances, I'd be elated. But captains are responsible, and someone who can't let her mom know where she is isn't someone I deem as responsible, Charli Black."

My mother was not letting up. She wanted to know where I was. Honestly, I was so caught up in being with Blake that I did not think whether my parents were worried. Maybe my mom had a

point. Maybe I'd been so self-centered that I was not really thinking about anybody but me, and that wasn't right.

"I was with Blake."

"Doing what and where?" my mom said, demanding an answer, hands on her hips. "You got out of practice two hours ago. Charli, you're going to wind up pregnant."

Shocked, I said, "Mom, no I'm not."

"So you weren't with that boy, kissing somewhere or doing much worse?"

Things were pretty intense with us in Blake's car. I couldn't lie to my mom. I just looked away.

"Charli?"

"We didn't go far, Mom. Okay? Blake respects me."

"I've seen Blake. He's gone from a skinny, little toothpick to a bodybuilder for goodness' sake. I know what high school boys want."

"But do you know what Daddy wants?" I mumbled under my breath

"What did you say?" my mom asked, looking like she wanted to strangle me.

"I'm just saying, Mom, you gotta learn how to trust me. I can handle my relationship.

But can you handle yours? I came in here, and you and Dad were fussing. I'm not trying to be disrespectful, but I am getting older. You can't treat me like a child. What's going on with y'all? What's going on with your husband?"

"Since you're so grown, you take your behind from my presence and ask him." I did not know what I'd done or said or how far I'd pushed her, but she screamed, "*Go!* Go ask him."

"What's going on in here?" my dad rushed in and asked.

"Talk to your daughter. She has some questions about your behavior. I think it's best you answer them, Mr. Integrity. And while y'all are at it, find something to eat tonight. I'm not cooking."

"Like that's surprising," my father said, before grabbing his keys. I followed Dad out the door.

My dad was the most refined man I knew. Classy and distinguished, he was never rattled and definitely believed not everything should be discussed. I knew he would not want me to talk about him and my mom. However, she had a point. If he was out doing things he shouldn't with someone else, then he was guilty. There

were consequences, like his daughter being up-set. Over the years I had come to understand the one thing my dad wanted to keep intact was my admiration. I was his princess. He didn't like me uncomfortable. He'd provided me with everything I'd ever asked for, unless my mom stepped into the picture and made him feel like he shouldn't oblige my every wish.

"Dad, do you still love Mom?" I said when the car was too quiet.

"Of course, I love your mom, sweetheart. You don't have to worry about anything. Honestly, we were having a serious discussion about you."

I didn't want to tell him what I'd heard. Though their conversation did start out with me, it ended up on him. What was he hiding?

Seeing I was puzzled, he flipped the focus. "Where were you, Charli?"

"I need a new phone, Daddy. My battery keeps dying, and I don't want to buy a new bat-tery that's gonna cost forty or fifty dollars when … I want a new phone. I've had this one for two years. I've been a good steward. Every time I charge it, it dies shortly thereafter."

"Why don't you go and get a new phone?"

"'Cause I have two more weeks before the two years is up, and Mom doesn't wanna pay the higher price."

He shrugged like that was stupid. "So where were you?"

"I was with my boyfriend."

"And I'm supposed to believe he doesn't have a phone?"

"He was just giving me a ride home, and we stopped off to briefly celebrate," I said, choosing my words carefully because I didn't want to tell a fib to my dad either.

I couldn't tell him everything though. If I said the wrong thing, I might not be able to see Blake again. Thinking back on Blake's love, I knew we could never be apart.

"Why didn't you just wait for your mom to come pick you up?"

"I'm going to the eleventh grade. I didn't want my mom to pick me up."

"So you'd rather hop into Hallie's unreliable car with your friends? That's crazy."

"You know her dad is a mechanic. It might not look like it can make it, but it's got all new parts."

"Still ... and then you are relying on some boy."

Knowing my father wanted me to have my own stuff, I said, "I need my own car. I've been telling y'all that but ..."

"There's no but. You're right. You need your own car."

Then my dad whipped the car into the BMW sales lot. Everything in me was sparkling. There was a small, shiny black, four-door sedan dazzling on the showroom floor.

"Do you like it?"

"Like it? I love it!" I uttered back, amazed.

We got the salesman to take it outside. When I test-drove it, I felt like I was flying. The automobile was flawless. Ninety minutes later, after all of the details were finalized, it was mine.

Driving it home, I realized I didn't get to press my dad about what was going on with him personally. I had a car of my own. My thoughts were diverted, plus my daddy told me that he loved my mom. I had to believe things were going to work out for them. Besides, that was their business. At this moment I could not let anything get me down. My relationship with

Blake was going great. I was now captain of the cheerleading squad, and I had the bomb ride.

As soon as we pulled up into our yard, I ran up to my dad and threw my arms around him. "I love you so much!"

My mom came outside and her mouth dropped. She was not pleased. But when I ran up to her and kissed her too, she didn't make him take it back. She was not happy at all.

"I'm gonna be responsible, Mom. I'm gonna keep my grades up. I'm gonna shoot for a three-point-seven-five or a four-point-o this year. You won't have to worry about anybody driving me home. I'll drive the speed limit. I'll obey all laws. Mom, I got a car!"

My dad came over to my mom. He told her I really needed the car. Then he handed her four one-hundred dollar bills.

She asked, "What's this for?"

"Money to go and get that child a new phone. Waiting two weeks is ridiculous when the one she has right now won't hold a charge."

Frustrated, she vented, "Whatever Charli wants, Charli gets, huh?"

My dad asserted, "Whatever she needs, she's going to get, yes."

"I … I … I can wait. I'll go charge my phone now," I said, not wanting my parents to argue.

"Can I take you guys on a ride? Please. Mom, come on, isn't he beautiful?"

"Your car?" my mom said, shaking her head.

"Yes. This is Sir Charles," I uttered, naming the beauty.

"Let me go change outta this suit, and I'll be right back," my dad said.

With my arms wrapped around my mom, I said, "Mom, please don't be mad."

"I just would've liked to discuss this with your dad. We'd already said we were gonna wait until second semester to get you a car, and he just goes out and does it." She looked away.

And then she brought my chin to hers and said, "But you are a good girl, and you deserve it. Sir Charles is beautiful. I'm happy for you."

She gave me a big hug. I was ecstatic. Having my mom's approval was major.

As I drove my brand new car, all was right with the world. Sir Charles was packed

to capacity with all my girls inside. We were following my parents to Hilton Head, South Carolina, and heading to a rented mansion for the weekend. I was determined to have a good time because as soon as we got back, it would be time for cheer camp. And school would soon follow. This was the last big break before my world was about to turn crazy.

I needed a serene moment. However, I didn't consider the Eva factor. She always had something smart to say, and this time was no different.

"I'm surprised you invited us. I thought we'd be kicked to the curb again for Blake," Eva said, obviously still as salty as movie popcorn.

I peeked in my rearview mirror and saw her rolling her eyes at me. A part of me wanted to pull over, right on an isolated stretch of Highway 16, and kick her out. But I couldn't. One, because I was following my parents. Two, because I didn't have it in me to ever be that cruel. Three, I knew deep down Eva cared but just didn't know how to show it.

Instead of getting upset, I made a caring gesture. "I'm sorry, you guys. I should've stuck to my word and gone with you guys the other day."

"You don't owe us any explanation," Ella said.

Randal said, "You wanted to celebrate with your guy. If any of us had a man, we'd be doing the same thing."

Eva was in a mood. "Speak for yourself, girl. I gotta man."

"Uh, one-night stands don't qualify as having a man," Hallie added.

"I know, right?" Randal said, as the two of them slapped hands.

Ella looked at her sister and said, "Don't even respond back because she's right. If you can't take the heat, you need to leave the pressing comb alone."

Everybody knew Eva was faster than the rest of us, but now it seemed all Eva cared about was being satisfied. Maybe this weekend would give us all the chance to talk to her so she could start off this year with a better reputation.

About an hour later, we were pulling up to the house in Wexford. It was a gated community with a country club, and the property we rented had five bedrooms, four baths, a swimming pool

right off the water, and a boat. My dad told us we would take it out a little later on in the evening.

My parents appeared happier. My goal for this weekend was for me to hang with my friends and allow them to have time to themselves to bond. We did not have to worry about cooking or cleaning because my mom had hired a maid and a caterer to do the job. We were to relax and be pampered. I certainly brought the right friends along for that.

As Ella, Hallie, Randal, and I relaxed on the beach, Eva strutted away.

"Why does she always have an attitude?" Hallie asked, saying what we all were thinking.

"There's just a lot going on with our family right now," Ella said. "She tries to act tough, but she doesn't know how to deal with it."

"Anything you wanna talk about?" Randal said.

"My dad's marrying his girlfriend. They already have one son, and now she's pregnant again.

"Eva just feels like it's a slap in our face. My dad didn't wanna raise us, but he's happy raising sons with this other lady."

"And did you tell them the other part?" Eva came up behind the four of us and said. "He has back child support due. My mama's struggling. He's playing house with somebody else. Just isn't right. I'm sorry, Charli, if I'm not happy you got a brand new car. I can't relax on the beach and enjoy this lavish house we're staying in when my world is not right. It's not all good for me, and I can't pretend that it is."

I got up, dusted some of the sand off, and said, "I'm not asking you to pretend, nor am I tryna flaunt anything in your face."

"You gotta admit," Hallie added, "your life is pretty together. My dad might be about something, but he's still a single parent. My mom is strung out on drugs somewhere, and every time I mention trying to find her and help her, he goes off."

"And it ain't cool being mixed either," Randal said. "My mom has no clue about my world or about my hair. My dad's so busy with work. Sometimes I wonder if he stays away so much because he's ashamed of his mixed family."

I so badly wanted to tell my friends that though my life looked like it was all together, it

wasn't. If they only huffed and puffed, my walls would come tumbling down too. I could not talk to them about my parents because they were with us this weekend. Besides, I didn't want anybody examining my crazy parents.

I had always been taught to keep my business to myself, but these were my girls. They thought I had it going on. Maybe it was better if one of us did because if we were all too messed up, who could hold us all together? Being the rock was my job.

I picked up a little sand and threw it below their waists. With black girls, you couldn't put sand in their hair because it wasn't like we were tryna get in the water. It would take a lot of effort to get out the sand. Plus my parents already said we were taking the boat out, and we were going to hang with other families who had vacationed with us for years.

"Watch the sand," Eva said. "We have enough to worry about. I don't want to add our hair to the list."

"That's right," Hallie said to her.

"We all need to relax and enjoy," I said. "We got each other, and we're going into the eleventh

grade. We're cheerleaders—varsity cheerleaders. We got a chance to win state on a competition squad. Forget boys. Forget problems. For the next couple of days, let's just have a real vacation."

That's exactly what we did. We rode bicycles. We went putt-putting. We took long walks on the beach. We slept in late, and we laughed ourselves silly. Looking out on that beautiful blue water, I wished things could just stay this way. I was just so happy. Blake was texting me, telling me how much he missed me. I had come up with some new moves that I knew were really going to make us competitive. My parents were really enjoying each other. Life was great. I was on cloud nine.

CHAPTER 3
Big Head

Oh, so you can't come and swoop me up after all the rides I've been giving you?" Blake asked, trying to make me feel guilty.

"Honey, it's not like I don't want to see you. Of course I'm going to give you a ride in the car, but I got to get to practice early. You've been captain for a while. Your dad gives you all the extras you need to make sure your team is on and popping, but me, I'm new at this. I want to get with Coach Woods, get her expectations, and be an example for my squad. Leadership starts at the top. So I can't pick you up today."

"Dang, give a girl some power and she loses her mind," Blake uttered. "I needed to talk to you."

As I sat on my bed putting on some lotion, I put the phone down and hit the speaker button. "See, you're tripping. Nothing about me has changed. Just because I'm taking my job seriously, you've got an issue with that. I didn't say anything when you had to go to the gym in the morning, watch film after that, lift weights in the afternoon, run around the track in the evening, and eat your food and mine because you're trying to gain all this weight so you can pass some eyeball test for scouts. Plus, you're there early on days you want to, so why can't I have my guy's support, huh?"

"I'm just playing. We can rap later. Dang, when you put it like that, go to practice. But take it from me, you don't want to be too hard on your girls, or they'll resent you."

"I hear you. But I can't be too soft on them either, or they'll think I'm a pushover. I got this."

Driving to practice, all I could think about was how happy I was that everything in my life was right. While I appreciated Blake giving me his advice on how to be a captain and not alienating my team, I did have to realize that girls and boys were different. I truly felt in my gut that if

I was too soft, we wouldn't accomplish anything. All they would want to do is chat and text and do everything but get us ready to win the state competition this December. This practice started the countdown, and while cheerleading might not mean the world to most people, it meant everything to me. I was not going to allow one girl on my team to be a slacker.

"Okay, so where is Coach Woods?" I uttered to myself when I pulled up to the gym an hour before practice and saw no cars in the parking lot.

We had already corresponded through e-mail. She knew I was planning to be there early. If her plans had changed, why didn't she text me? Corresponding was only right. It was only responsible. And I knew she would expect it of me. Coach or not, I expected it out of her. When my cell phone rang, I thought Coach was reading my mind. However, when I looked at my new cell, it wasn't Coach at all. It was Randal.

I said, "Hey, girl. Are you on your way to practice?"

"No, we got fifty minutes."

"Well, you want to make your way over here. You don't want to be late," I told her.

"Well, that's what I was calling for, to see if you wanted to come swoop me up."

"Ha-ha, no, honey. You should have gotten with me beforehand. I'm already at practice."

"How can you be at practice?" she questioned. "It hasn't started yet."

"I'm the captain, remember? There are things that I need to do with Coach before you guys even get here. I mean, I wouldn't have had any problem bringing you with me. You could have warmed up, and you know, learned some cheers or something. All the extra practice is great, but I can't leave now to come and pick you up. Sorry. You should have called me earlier," I reiterated a second time.

Tired of me, she gasped, "Okay, I got it."

Thirty minutes later, twenty minutes before practice was supposed to start, Coach Woods still wasn't there. I was pacing back and forth in front of the gym door, wondering where in the world she was. There was no way I could conduct practice outside if she didn't show up. I could not start late because I valued my squad's time, and JV practiced after us.

Five minutes later, I saw her car pull into the parking lot. I didn't even give her time to get out.

I quickly ran up and said, "Coach Woods, where have you been? Practice is about to start in a few minutes, and we had planned for you to be here a long time ago. I need to get your cell number right away because the only numbers I had were your home and your office number. I called both several times. I was thinking maybe somebody might have dropped you off even though I didn't see any cars. Where have you been? Why didn't you call me?"

"Okay, Charli Black, you're excited. You're dedicated. I see that you're on point. Could you give me a chance to answer one of your questions before you keep rambling? An emergency came up with my child at daycare, and I had to go by and take care of all that. Is that okay with you? I lost power in my phone, so I couldn't call you. I got here as soon as I could."

When she mentioned power being lost in her phone, I couldn't get too upset because I had just got a new phone for that very reason. The

barracuda in me calmed down. I became more like the loving koala.

In a sweeter tone, I asked, "Is your child okay?"

"Yes, thank you."

She was taking her time getting out of the car, and I said, "Can I help you get inside the gym? The girls will be here in a minute, and I want to have the mats set up."

"But it's everybody's job to help put out the mats."

"Yes, and it also takes extra time to do that, so I figured if different girls would rotate and come a couple minutes early to practice, the mats would be ready to go. We wouldn't lose any time."

Squinting, she looked at me and said, "It's hard to get people to come on time, Charli, much less come early."

"Coach, my squad, my rules. Feel like if we all have some ownership and make a little sacrifice, we'll give more, and we'll compete harder. And at the end of the day, you'll be smiling when we win. Can we at least try it before you say it won't work? Please?"

"Sure. You're ambitious; I'll definitely give you that. And Whitney thought you wouldn't have any backbone. I have a feeling that her opinion is *way* off base."

I had the mats all ready to go with one minute to spare because Coach Woods helped me. When it was time for practice, only two girls were on time. They were sophomores Chrissy and Hunter. The other three sophomores were nowhere to be found, nor were my friends or the seniors.

Five minutes passed. I stood in the doorway and saw Hallie's car pull up. It was jerking, and smoke was coming out of the back. It made it though, and my four girlfriends got out as soon as it came to a stop.

Hallie ran up to me and smiled. "Hey, captain! We're here and ready for a great practice."

"Hey, Charli." Ella tried to give me five, but I did not put my hand up.

With a little attitude, Randal said, "Sorry we're late. They had to come pick me up because somebody wouldn't."

I rolled my eyes. I was not smiling. This was practice time, and I felt they were not taking my leadership seriously.

Eva looked at me and said, "Okay, what's up your butt? You better pull it out before you stay constipated."

"You guys are late, okay," I said to her in a brash tone.

"Whatever. Where's the rest of this squad? There's got to be some kind of grace period. Right, Coach Woods?" Eva yelled out.

But Coach Woods was on the phone with the daycare center, so she didn't hear Eva. The four of them saw I was seriously disappointed. They should have been on time.

"I get to discipline anyone who does not follow the rules. It's unacceptable that you guys were late for any reason. Go stretch and be prepared to do some laps when everyone gets here."

"Oh heck nah!" Eva said before Ella and Randal pulled her back.

It wasn't until twenty minutes later that the whole squad was there, and I quickly said, "Everybody's running ... everybody except me, Chrissy, and Hunter. We were the only three here on time."

"I'm not doing any jogging," Whitney came up to me and said.

Not backing away, I stood my ground. "If you want to stay on this squad, you will!"

I heard tons of groans. Since they had attitudes and didn't appreciate what I was trying to instill, I had to punish them. It was not until they ran twenty times around the gym that I said stop. I got all kinds of dirty looks, but I knew it would be worth it when we won the trophy. I ran this team, and they were going to respect that. I bet they would be on time to all other practices.

"Okay, everything is just right. Thank you, Mom, for letting me have a swim party over here for my team."

My mom said, "Well, you tricked me on this one because you know I don't like last minute surprises."

"I know, I know. But I've been really hard on them this week. I haven't heard from Hallie and the girls. I know they're upset with me."

"You're not being rude to your girlfriends, are you?"

"No, but I mean ... look at it from my point of view, they were sort of taking advantage of me being the captain. It was like them thinking

because we're tight and all, I'm not going to hold them accountable. They elected me. They should have known how I'd be."

I could tell by her face that my mom thought I was too over the top. "That might just be it. You might be acting differently than what they expected you to be acting like," she said.

I thought my mom was wrong. My team needed a tough leader. Being in charge was not easy, but you must be willing to do whatever it takes to get dynamic results. I was willing. This party was proof.

The doorbell rang and before I could answer it, my mom said, "Charli, just remember to treat people as you would want to be treated."

"Yes, ma'am. I want a leader that's on it. I hear you. I'm with that. I got this, Mom," I said, needing her to ease up.

Walking to the door seemed to take forever. I couldn't understand why everyone was telling me to ease up. We were not just pom-pom girls. Cheerleading was a sport. We were expected to be winners. If I did not demand their full commitment to our practices and the rules of the team, then how could I expect them to deliver

excellence in their performances? If I held back from wanting them to give me their best, then I felt like I would be doing them an injustice. And that just wasn't in me.

"Hey, come on in."

Balancing her keys and bag in one hand and her slushy in the other, Hallie said, "Hey, girl!"

"Be careful with the punch," I said to the four of them when I looked at their lidless Quik Trip cups.

"You want us to take our shoes off too?" Eva said, flaring her nose.

I said, "Don't trip. You know the rules of my mom's house. Yes, take off your shoes."

My friends could not blame me because my parents took care of the things we had. Other people had junky rooms, junky cars, and junky houses because they just allowed people to abuse their stuff. That was not the way it was for my family. I was not going to allow anybody to make me feel bad because we had standards. But of course Eva looked at me like I was speaking another language, so I bent down, picked up one of her feet, took off her flip-flop, and frowned when I saw her unpolished toenails.

"Don't you trip," she said to me. "Everybody doesn't have money to go to the spa, all right?"

"We figure out a way to do what we want. I have some of that ninety-nine cent fingernail polish upstairs. You can have the whole bottle."

Randal then pulled me aside and said, "Okay, do you have to be such a brat? Did you forget Ella and Eva are going through some things? Lay off of them."

Remembering their dad had a new family, I eased up. "Okay, I'm sorry guys. You know I'm just a little tense with the squad coming over. Thanks for getting here early. I need y'all to play hostess for me."

"Why should we help you out when you haven't been helping us out in practice?" Eva said. "And you've been treating us just like everybody else, so if you are rolling out the red carpet for the rest of the team, you need to be rolling out the red carpet for us."

Eva sashayed into my house, and the other three followed behind her, not wanting to assist me. The doorbell rang. I just threw up my hands and was like, *Whatever*!

To the back of my girls' heads I yelled, "You know how to get out to the pool. Just do whatever."

I'd been there for them countless times. I went overboard helping Hallie learn cheers for tryouts. I would give Eva and Ella dollars to buy the latest threads. I helped Randal understand black culture anytime she had a question, which was often. They could treat me cruel.

"Hey, girls," I said to the sophomore crew when I opened the door.

The two who were always on time, Chrissy and Hunter, were smiling and happy. The other three frowned at me like I was the wicked stepmother or something.

Just as I'd left the girls at the pool, my cell vibrated. I looked down and saw that it was Blake.

I quickly answered and said, "Hey, baby!"

"Hey, girl. Wassup? We hanging out tonight or what? You been putting me off for all this cheerleading stuff. It's our time, right? I get that ride you promised me earlier in the week?"

"I thought I told you ..."

"You thought you told me what? What time you were picking me up?" he asked, starting to get an attitude.

"No, I thought I told you the cheerleading squad was coming over here for a little swim party."

"Oh! You ain't said nothing but a word. The boys will be over in just a minute."

"No, no, no. My mom said guys can't come. It's just for the girls to bond. It's not going to be that long. We'll hook up later, okay?"

"You putting me off again? Come on now. I need to share something. You know I need a little bit of loving ... affection ... something."

"Blake, the pressure is not fair," I said, irritated with all his whining. "Just like you're trying to win a state title, well, I'm trying to as well."

"Yeah, but football isn't on twenty-four-seven for me, so cheerleading shouldn't be for you either."

I didn't want to sit there and baby him. However, I sensed his stress. Just when I was about to help him understand I wasn't putting him off, the doorbell rang.

Needing him to deal with it, I quickly said, "I gotta go."

The senior crew came in, and they had their minds fixed on swimming. It was seven o'clock,

and it was still ninety-two degrees. My city was not called Hotlanta for nothing.

"I thought before you guys swim, we could have a quick cheer meeting," I announced. I got several eyes rolls in my direction. "Okay, fine. You all can swim. I have snacks here too. But in twenty minutes, we're going to have a meeting."

Well, that didn't go over well. I pushed it back to thirty minutes, but that was my absolute limit. I just kept walking around making sure everyone was having a good time. I was trying to meet girls on the team. I was trying to loosen up. I was trying to be approachable, but they kept doing stupid stuff like running around the pool. What if they hurt themselves? Though my parents had insurance, who wanted to go through that hassle? More importantly, I could not afford to lose a cheerleader for our upcoming training.

We were about to have choreography camp next week, and everyone needed to be healthy. I saw a couple of the girls already eating a few too many hot dogs, so I told them to pull back. They looked at me like I was being rude. But I was just trying to help.

One of the girls on the squad had a really stylish bathing suit on, which was also too small. I went over and said to her, "I changed the size of your uniform order. When it comes in, it was the size that was ordered and not a mistake. We can't have all of our business hanging out, you know."

I actually hated hearing myself talk like that because it felt like I was my mom, but somebody had to be the adult, the rational one, the leader, and that was me. I went inside to find a whistle because I need to get their attention. I did not have a whistle, but my dad had one. He used to coach my softball team when I was little, and he never threw anything away. I knew exactly where it was in his desk. But as I started to walk back outside from my dad's office, I was surprised to see Whitney talking to Hallie and Eva in the kitchen.

"So this is what you guys wanted as a leader instead of me? I'm telling you, we've got to do something about it, or she's going to drive all of us crazy. Charli's your friend. You need to figure out a way to tell her to chill out, or else we're all going to go to the coach and get her removed."

Honestly, something I was doing was not working, but then I thought that maybe they were just jealous. Certainly Hallie and Eva would have my back. But maybe I was kidding myself because Eva said, "You're right. We got to do something about her."

I ducked back inside the office before they saw me. I was losing the team, even though I had gone out of my way to throw them a party. Plus I was doing all I could to make sure they were sharp. I had to think. I had to keep it together. I could not get all emotional and cry and beg for them to like me. It was just tough on them, but like any good solider that makes it through boot camp, they'd appreciate it in the end, or at least I hoped they'd appreciate *me* in the end. Gosh, being a leader was hard.

"You realize I've lost count of how many times this week that you've told me no," Blake said, a little upset with me when I told him I was going to practice instead of hanging out with him.

"Not because I want to, but we have practice."

"Well, we're off today. Maybe I'll come up there and watch you."

"Blake, it's not like you can do that. Coach is strict. Our practice is closed. Plus if you were there, you know I wouldn't be able to concentrate and neither would half of my team because they all think you're fine," I said, stoking his ego on purpose.

"All right, all right, you got me there," he said, grinning.

I pleaded, "Let me just get through choreography camp. We're going to have our time."

"Is it going to be worth my while ... all this waiting you're making me do?"

"Yes, yes, yes," I said, in a sultry, slow voice.

"All right then."

"Why are you talking to that boy on the phone in that manner?" My mom came into my room, startling me and interrupting the last part of my conversation.

I hung up on Blake. I knew that would get under his skin. But I did hope he heard my mom talking in the background because I didn't want him to be too salty.

"Mom, you don't need to be eavesdropping," I said, trying to divert her thoughts. Her stern look told me she wasn't going to steer away from the sex talk. "I'm a junior in high school. I have

a boyfriend who's committed to me. I mean, honestly, Mom. We haven't talked about this, but I got to keep him."

"So what does that mean? You are just going to do anything and everything he asks? And where do you think that's going to lead? You give him an inch, and he'll want a mile."

"I don't understand what that means, Mom."

"It means that if you're only trying to please Blake, and he doesn't care about your values and morals, then it is never going to be enough. He's always going to want more. You'll get hurt."

I just wanted to scream, "That's probably why you and Dad are having problems right about now." But I knew there was no way I could go there with my mom. I did want to keep my two front teeth. However, maybe that's what she needed me to say. Maybe I needed to be real with her and call a spade a spade. Calling a spade a spade were words she used all the time. She needed to be concerned about satisfying her guy because it was obvious that she didn't have a clue. Which didn't give her a lot of credibility in handing out advice about men.

"Why are you looking at me like that, Charli? Like you pity me or something. I am older and wiser and have been where you are about to go. These little boys tell you what you want to hear. You young girls give it up too soon and end up wishing you hadn't or worse—pregnant or with a disease or something."

Frustrated, I uttered, "Mom, I got to go to practice. I don't want a lecture."

"Maybe what I need to do is take the keys from you, and then you'll have time to listen to what I have to say. You're getting way too grown-up."

"Okay, Mom. I'm sorry. I'm sorry. I'm listening," I said, definitely not wanting my independence to be taken from me. Being rational, I said, "Just so you know, I told Blake I'm not ready."

"Yeah, but I also heard you on the phone. Actions speak louder than words. It was something in your voice. Something in the way your little body was moving while you were on the telephone. It just makes me think you're getting a little ahead of yourself. And you know what? After practice, come straight home. You're not seeing him tonight."

"I didn't want to see him tonight, Mom. I'll be dead tired from choreography camp. I'm with you. I've got big dreams ahead. I'm not going to mess up my life. It's all good, okay?" I looked at my watch. "Can I go now, please? I don't want to be late."

She stuck out her cheek for me to kiss. "Bye," she said.

I met Eva at the door to the gym twenty minutes later. "Somebody's not so early to practice today," she smirked.

"I'm not in charge today since we have a choreographer," I uttered, wanting her to know if I had other duties I would have been there earlier.

"Good," she said, clearly alluding to the fact that she was sick of my leadership.

I didn't even want to respond because I owed her no apology. I owed none of them any apologies. I was doing what was necessary. I was doing what was right. I was doing what they needed, and she just needed to deal with it.

The choreographer was hip, and after she gave us her background, I was really impressed. She was straight from New York, and had hip-hop, classical, jazz, and tap training.

"Everyone, I'm Brenda Bill. I'm only here for two days. The routine is super tough, and I don't go at a kindergartner's pace. If you keep your lips closed, your eyes on me, and your feet moving, you can get this. We'll add the music to it after we're done. Hands up in the air, clap, clap, one, two, three, four, five, six, seven, eight."

She went down. She turned around. She jumped in the air. She stepped back and then she repeated the eight-count. On the third time, I had the dance. Everyone else was looking as if they were in preschool and the routine she was doing was for college girls.

"Okay, okay, hold up, hold up," Brenda said, frowning at the other girls' awful adaptation of her routine. She pointed to me. "What's your name?"

"Charli."

Brenda came over to me and patted me on the back. "Everyone needs to be dancing like Charli. Her movements are on point. Watch her. Go, Charli."

I started doing the eight-count.

"Perfect precision!" she turned to everyone else. "I can't keep stopping. You guys are going

to have to work on this on your own. I have got to keep moving. Maybe you can get with Charli if you don't have it on your own time."

As the day went on, I was the only one who had the routine down. The next day was more of the same. I tried to get with girls offline, but they said they had it. They recorded Brenda on their phones. I assumed they went home and practiced. I don't know why they bothered recording her because they came back the second day worse than they were at the end of day one.

When our time with her was over, Brenda called us all in and said, "Thank goodness she's the captain because she's the only one who has it. Straight up, seriously, if you guys are trying to win any competition this year, you are going to have to work like her. Go home, practice, get in front of the mirror, look at yourselves, straighten up, and want this. Be upbeat."

Brenda went over and talked to Coach Woods. She had to turn in all the formations on a spreadsheet so we would know where we were supposed to go as we practiced. I was left there with a deflated team. They looked like they were all hit in the gut.

To pep them up I said, "This isn't easy, you guys. We all wanted to be on this team. Brenda's right. If we're going to win, we have to give extra. I hate that you guys are mad at me. But instead of hating on me, you need to be hating the pitiful effort you guys were giving. If you had it like I do, we'd be a mile ahead right now and could be sharpening up the routine. As it stands, I'll have to reteach it all next week. It's not my preference to be tough, but I'd rather be tough than pitiful."

Whitney said, "Eva, you better get your friend."

Eva shouted out with attitude, "Oh, don't worry. We're definitely doing something because somebody's got the big head."

CHAPTER 4

Reality Check

So, Eva, do you have anything you want to say to me? Saying that I have a big head? I mean … really?" I said aloud to someone who I thought was my girl.

"Read whatever into it you want, Charli," Eva said while her neck rolled back at me.

There's lots of oohs and ahhs going on all around me. I didn't want to have a big blowup with Eva. Honestly, I was tired of her mouth. If she had something to say, we needed to discuss it. So when Brenda came back over to have the team do it one more time, I asked Eva if I could see her offline. I was shocked when she said no. As we did the number, the pep in my step that

I'd had over the last two days waned. It was not that I did not know what to do, but in my mind I was so frustrated, so off guard, and so caught off track that my body could not keep up.

Brenda came over to me and said, "Okay, uh … Maybe I bragged on you too soon, Charli Black. I just love your name, though. I think it's so cool. But bring it for me now."

"You definitely bragged on her too soon," Whitney said. She had a coy grin, obviously happy I was not perfect.

I dashed to the locker room. My plan of being hard on the team may have backfired on me. The tough skin I thought I had was thinner than I wanted. It was difficult to endure their hard glares and mean stares. All of this was getting to me. Now I understood the phrase, "no man is an island," because I did not want to be alone. When the team came in to collect their things, that's exactly what I was.

Not even Hallie and Ella were talking to me. What had I done? It actually hurt my heart when I was sitting alone on the bench, feeling a little down, and I knew my crew saw me. But they kept to themselves, laughed a little bit, and headed out

without saying anything. With my head bowed, I did not see mean-girl Whitney approaching.

Whitney leaned in my ear and taunted me. "Guess someone is realizing they're not all that after all. You can't treat people like dogs and expect them to worship you."

"You'd know," I snapped, knowing that there was no love lost between us. I did not want to let her think that she was getting to me, and though her words did not feel good, I was determined not to break. So I gathered my stuff, headed to my car, and immediately called Blake.

"Where are you, baby? I need to see you," I said to him, but it was loud in the background.

Blake kept saying, "Hello, hello."

Usually he knew it was me calling because he could see my name on the caller ID, but he was probably so preoccupied and distracted that he pressed the answer button without looking at the screen. Whatever it was, he did not know it was me. I needed him though, so he had to listen.

I yelled into the receiver. "It's Charli. I wanna come give you a ride. Let's see each other. Where are you?"

"That's not gonna work for me right now. I'm out. I can't hear you. Okay, hit me back a little later. Bye, Charli." Blake hung up.

When I got home, I dialed Hallie, and she didn't answer. I called Ella, and she didn't respond either. I knew I wasn't calling Eva, so I tried Randal.

"Hey," I said in a tone that was real sweet. I used it because I didn't want to offend her.

Randal said, "Hey, Charli ... um ... I can't really talk because I'm about to head out."

"Cool, y'all going somewhere? I wanna come."

Randal was timid, but she still was direct. "I'm not driving."

"I can drive. I know Hallie's car has been having some issues, so I can scoop you guys up."

"You're on speaker!" Hallie yelled out in the background. "My car's just fine. My dad's a mechanic, remember? He wouldn't have me driving something that was gonna fall apart any minute."

She and I both knew that wasn't true— I mean her dad *is* a mechanic, and her car is not going to explode. However, that car was a hunk of junk no matter how many parts were

replaced. Unless it had been in his shop within the last forty-eight hours, they were taking a chance on it stalling out somewhere.

"I was just saying," I softly replied, backing away from my last statement.

"What do you want?" Eva called out in haste.

Ticked, I blurted, "Thanks, Randal, for letting me know I'm on speaker."

"Were you gonna talk about us or something?" Eva questioned.

"No, I don't do that," I said. "Unlike others I thought I could trust."

"Oh, true. You don't talk about us or to us until your little feelings get hurt. Then you're calling everybody. Except me because you know I ain't tryna hear it. You better call Blake. Maybe he's got time for you."

Then I heard laughter in the background. I could not believe they were giggling about this. My life was falling apart, and they thought it was funny.

"All right, fine. See you guys," I said, fed up.

I wasn't going to beg anybody to hang out with me. They knew I loved them. I might have been a little brash, but that did not mean I did

not have feelings, that I did not care about them, and that they should just treat me any old kind of way.

Eva did have a point though. I needed to get with Blake. I needed to be in his arms. I needed him to hold me. I needed him to tell me everything was going to be okay. He had been the captain of his team as a sophomore. He'd been through all this, and I hadn't listened to him before when he was trying to tell me how to respond and how to not be too rough. Now I was definitely going to listen because my way clearly was not working.

The call went straight to his voicemail, so I texted him. Twenty minutes later, I called him again. Fifteen minutes later, I texted him again. He was not calling me back. I knew he needed me over the last few days, and I could not be there. I still did not know what he wanted to discuss. I just hoped I could find him and bond with him in the way he had been waiting for.

I was going nuts pacing back and forth in my room, wondering where in the world was Blake. Why wasn't he picking up my calls? I desperately

needed to be with him just like a person who'd been in the desert for days without water longed for a drink. I just needed to speak to him, talk to him, hear his voice, or something. The non-communication was truly unsettling.

I picked up my phone and called him one more time. When his voicemail came on I said, "Blake, this is my tenth time calling or maybe the eleventh. I don't know what's going on. I only know that you're not answering the phone. Where are you? What's wrong?"

Then I decided to just get my keys and go find him. I went into my mom's room to ask if I could head out, but her door was locked. I knocked on it and heard her moaning.

"You okay, Mom?" When she didn't respond I asked, "Is it okay if I head out for a little while? I'll be right back."

In an upset tone, she said, "Just be careful and make sure you're in this house before eleven-thirty."

It was nine, but I had to take what I could get, so I said, "Yes, ma'am."

When I got in Sir Charles, I started thinking as if I was Blake. Where would he be? One place I

knew I needed to hit was the bowling alley. Blake and some of his teammates loved going there to talk junk and try to beat each other. It also had a video arcade, laser tag, and it was just a cool place where they liked to hang out. However, his car was nowhere in sight. I didn't even go in to look.

The skating rink was not too far away, but I didn't think he was there, as it was old folk's night. However, I could not rule it out until I got there. But my instincts were right; his car was not there either.

I did an immediate U-turn. While I loved my car to pieces, this was one time I couldn't wait to find his. I wanted him to drive me around in his car, look over at me with his gorgeous eyes, recline in his passenger seat, and allow the moment to sweep us away. Where was he?

Then I drove to the strip where all the restaurants were. I did a double take when I saw my father coming out of a fancy restaurant with a lady I'd never seen. She was laughing, and she had her hands on his back. Quickly, I took both hands off the steering wheel while I clutched my heart. It just started burning. I felt like I could

not breathe. It was as if someone was holding me underwater, and I wanted to come up for air. Finally, when I saw him open his car door for her and kiss her hand, I gasped.

I screamed out, "Dad!"

Of course my windows were rolled up, and he could not hear me. This was so unfair. My mom had been fussing with him about something, and I thought it was all her fault. However, no woman makes a man cheat. He could at least have the decency to end it with my mom before he moved on.

As I had seen people do in detective movies and television shows, I followed them. Suddenly, two cars got in front of me, and I lost my father. But I couldn't shake the vision of him kissing someone else. Even though it was a hand, he was smiling too wide for it to be innocent. He was a jerk.

Needing a milkshake, which always made me feel better, I pulled into Zaxby's. I did not want to go in. I needed to find my father and Blake, but I was shaking too much. So I decided to take a break and went inside. But the line was too long, so I went to a booth and sat there.

"You okay, Charli?" a familiar voice said to me. I looked up and was surprised to see Brenton. I could only nod. "You are not all right. I'ma get you some water."

Before I could say, "No, thank you. I'm all right. I got it." He had gone and was back. And I was still not all right. I could not even drink the water. He was dressed in a Zaxby's uniform and had a broom in his hand. He sat down on the other side of the booth.

Brenton said, "What's wrong?"

"My life's just falling apart," I blurted out to my boyfriend's cousin.

Brenton and I went way back to elementary school. We used to be best buddies. When his cousin moved here in the ninth grade with his family, we drifted apart, like fall leaves blowing in the wind. I was his cousin's girl, and I now knew that hanging out with boys wasn't as good as hanging out with my girls. So we just lost touch. Knowing that he cared about me deep down, made me ready to open up.

"It's Blake, huh?" Brenton said.

"What? What do you know? What ... what aren't you telling me?"

"I'm just asking. I don't know anything. I haven't even talked to him since practice."

"I can't find him. But even as scared as I am about what's going on with him and where he is, I got bigger issues right now."

"I'm listening."

"I don't understand men. Can you explain that to me, Brenton? Why do you guys cheat?"

Boldly he said, "All men aren't dogs."

"Yeah, some are snakes."

"But girls don't want nice guys. They want the popular, crazy dudes."

"I'm not even talking about girls and boys now. I'm talking about grown men with families."

"I don't know. I've asked myself that time and time again. My dad left my mom before I was born."

Wanting to hit myself for not being sensitive, I said, "That's right."

It was already bad enough that I felt bad. I certainly did not want company in my misery. I remembered hearing that Brenton's father had skipped out before Brenton was born.

"It's cool. Coach, my mom's brother, is a great father figure. He's a good man and husband."

"Well," I immediately said, "don't go giving my father any accolades."

"What? Something's wrong at your house?"

Replaying the awful ordeal over again, I said, "I just saw my dad with another woman."

"Oh snap," Brenton said with a frown.

"Maybe I shouldn't have told you that. You won't say anything, right?" I gave Brenton a stern look.

"I never said anything about any of the stuff we shared." Brenton looked serious.

Finally figuring out where he was going with that comment, I said, "Oh, you mean when you kissed me in the closet in sixth grade?"

"No, when *you* kissed *me*."

We just laughed. I couldn't believe he had me laughing. My old buddy sure knew what I needed.

Then all of a sudden, I started crying. Brenton came on the other side of the booth and draped his arm around me as my head collapsed on his shoulder. Blake was not answering my calls. He was out doing his thing—his cousin knew it; I knew it. Something just wasn't right. My dad was doing his

thing too. My mom was in her room locked away—she knew it; I knew it. Something just wasn't right. My girls were out having a good time, not wanting to hang out with me—they knew it; I knew it. Something just wasn't right. I wasn't clueless, but I had no idea how to stop this wrong.

Sobbing, I said, "I'm so sorry, Brenton. I'm sorry. I'ma mess. I'm crying in your arms. What am I doing? Oh my gosh. Forgive me."

"No, no. It's okay," Brenton said. He gave me a comforting squeeze.

I was starting to feel so safe that I had to pull back because it just felt too awkward. I certainly did not want to give Brenton the wrong idea. I did not need to give myself anything extra to think about. When his phone that he had placed on the table started vibrating, I glanced at it and saw Blake's name. Before Brenton even knew what hit him, I answered it.

"What time you getting off work, cuz? You gotta come over to Bay's. The party's slamming."

I hung up on Blake before Brenton could say anything. Steam was piping from my ears. I

was livid! He was partying without me. I had to confront him immediately.

"Why you answer my phone like that?"

"Why are you tryna protect your cousin?" I said to him. "Who is Bay and where does she live?"

"Oh, he went to *that* party," Brenton said, trying to act like he didn't know.

"Are you going? You guys are about to close."

"I don't have a car."

"Problem solved because I've got one."

"Well, that's probably why Blake called because he was supposed to be here to pick me up."

"So you *knew* he was supposed to connect with you?" I said to Brenton, hitting him in the arm for being evasive earlier. "Text him and let him know you're covered."

"It's just a party. It's no big deal. You don't have to get all mad at Blake, make accusations, and come up with stuff all in your head. Let it go."

"I wanna go to the party. Will you take me or not?"

"You're the one with the car."

"I mean, will you let me drive you there or not? I can drop you off and not even come in."

"You would do that?" he said, looking at me now like I was being evasive by not being accurate about my intentions.

Actually, I did not even realize I was committing to something. I just said what I hoped would make him show me the way. I hoped he'd feel sorry for me and not hold me to what I said. If fibbing was what it was going to take for him to chill out and let me drive him to the party, then sure, fine, no big deal.

"Yes, I will just drop you off," I said, looking him square in the eyes.

I had to wait in the restaurant parking lot for him to actually get off from work. He had some clean-up chores he had to do. It made me really realize that not everybody had it like me. I did not have to work. I had a brand new car. But maybe my parents did not really value our family. As I sat there waiting on Brenton, I just reflected on what I saw earlier. Was I imagining the whole thing? Was my dad into this other woman? I did not want to call the house and ask if he was home because if my mom grilled me about my questions, I would have to spill the beans and let her know what I saw. And there

was no way I could do that because I couldn't break her heart. At nine-thirty at night, there was no explanation for another lady to be in my father's car other than hanky-panky. Seriously, that was just wrong.

I heard a tap on my window. It startled me. I didn't even realize my eyes were closed.

When I unlocked the door, Brenton said, "You always need to be checking out your environment, girl."

As he handed me a shake, I said, "Wow, thank you. You didn't steal it, did you?"

"I work here. I get discounts. I do have dollars. I figured you're giving me a ride that's the least I can do. I figured that's what you came in for. You used to always get a shake to make yourself feel better. I remembered strawberry cheesecake was your favorite flavor. It hasn't changed, has it?" Brenton asked, fully concerned about me.

"No," I said, appreciating his thoughtfulness. "So if I ask you what's really up with Blake, would you tell me or would it be this male loyalty thing?"

He huffed. I certainly did not want him to go back down the road of: *I don't know why you*

like him. Can't you just give me a try? Things were fine before he even moved here. You were supposed to be my girl. Blah, blah, blah, blah.

It was not that I wasn't sensitive or that Brenton was not adorable. It was just that ... Blake was fine. Blake was mine, and I wanted things to stay that way. Brenton was quiet, and it was probably best for things to be that way. I'd already cried on the guy's shoulder, for goodness' sake. I did not need to bare any more of my soul.

I was intrigued when he offered me an answer to an earlier question without me asking again. "Us guys just need to feel important sometimes. We just need girls to be there all the time when we call. I think it's probably the same for older men. I'm not saying your mom's not as amazing as you are, because I'm sure you get it from somewhere."

I backhand popped him in the arm because Brenton was so sweet. It was the first time I thought that if I wasn't with Blake maybe we could have something. He sure knew how to make me feel appreciated.

I continued to listen as he said, "If your dad is doing anything, it's probably because he feels like this other lady is there for him."

He did not have to say anything more at that point. I could connect the dots. Then he told me which direction to turn to get into Bay's subdivision. I realized that Blake probably had been telling his cousin that lately, I was unavailable. Obviously, Brenton was telling me that in Blake's mind that was unacceptable.

I had to fix this. I was thinking that I'd pull up, drop Brenton off, tell him to go and get Blake, and just believe that my beau was going to want to talk to me, hear me out, accept my apology, and all that. However, when I saw Blake outside, leaning against his car with his arms around Jackie's waist and her arms around his neck, laughing that same crazy way that my dad was doing earlier, I clutched my heart again. The laughter that I'd witnessed twice in one night seemed too illegal and immoral to be real. These men were supposed laugh that way only with the ladies they were committed too. Not other ones.

I stopped the car right in the middle of the street, jumped out, and said, "What in the

world is going on here? Get your hands off my man right now! Blake, what is this? I've been calling you and calling you. Obviously, nothing's wrong with your phone because you called your cousin."

"Man," Blake said to Brenton while he ignored me. "You were with Charli? You told her where I was and stuff? Man, what's up, cuz?"

"Don't even get mad at him. This is between us," I said, moving Blake's face to mine.

"Well, since he hasn't taken your calls," Jackie said, looking like the tramp she always dressed as, "that means he's through. He's not interested. He doesn't want to be around you."

My eyes started to well up, but I had to stay calm. "Blake, can I talk to you, please? This is between you and me."

"Go ahead and talk to her," Jackie said as Blake looked at her like he needed permission or something.

"Man, you don't even need to do the girl like this," Brenton said to Blake.

"You need to stay outta my business and give somebody a warning next time. Dang," Blake said, shoving Brenton out of the way.

Brenton stepped up to Blake as if he was defending my honor, and I pushed Brenton out the way. "Please, Brenton, let me talk to Blake. I have to fix this, please."

Brenton threw up his hands. I knew he was hurt. He walked into the party and did not look back.

It took Blake no time to tell me, "Oh, now you wanna come around and act like we're a couple and stuff? I've been tryna get with you for a couple of weeks. Things have been hard for my family, and I had no Charli to lean on. All you had time for was cheerleading."

Defending myself, with a cracking voice I said, "Yeah, it's not like I was with another guy or something."

"Oh no? You come strolling up in here with my cousin, and you're supposed to make me think that it's nothing?"

"No, there's nothing going on. You know that. Brenton would never, nor would I ever. What are you talking about? Don't turn this around," I said.

"You know what? There's no need to explain.

We're through. I'm with Jackie now. She's some-one who always has time for me."

When he walked away from me, he went into a Jackie's arms. She looked back and gave me a sly smile as they strolled away. My heart was racing.

I lost my friends, possibly my dad, and surely my man. I'd gone from the mountaintop to the valley. Where was Charli Black? If I didn't know it before, I knew it now. My life was hor-rible. What a reality check.

CHAPTER 5

Payback Hurts

It surely did not feel good seeing Blake leave me. The fact that we were through was bad enough, but to see him with another girl just felt ten times worse. We had to fix this.

I jogged over to him and said, "Please, Blake, please don't let this be over. You love me. Come on."

Surprisingly, Jackie said, "Talk to her."

Even she must have known we had something deeply special. I actually thought she would completely leave the scene, but she just stood there with her arms folded. I had to take what I could. I had another opportunity to get

Blake to see we were meant to be together. It was our time. It was supposed to be me and him, no one else. Whatever he was mad at me about, I could fix it.

"Charli, this isn't you. Don't beg. Don't follow me. Don't try to change my mind."

"But you don't know what you're doing. You really want us. I know you do," I continued, making my case as if I was a lawyer.

"Doesn't feel good, does it?" he asked coldly while Jackie gave me a hard glare.

"No, this doesn't feel right," I uttered when I placed my hands on his face.

He pulled away and lashed out at me, absolutely breaking my heart when he shouted, "I said we're through. When I needed you to be there, you had other stuff going on. Now that I've moved on, you gonna try and make time for me? How many times do I have to tell you no?"

"Blake, please."

I just fell to my knees, not caring that they might get scratched up—for a cheerleader to have yucky legs was for sure taboo. None of that mattered because in the pit in my stomach, I

was dying. I closed my eyes. When I felt strong arms around me, I leapt to my feet and said, "I knew you cared!"

"I never stopped caring," Brenton said to me, making me step back some from his arms.

I just took both of my hands and hit him in his chest repeatedly. "Why? Why? Why?"

Others from the party were now surrounding me. Folks were laughing. I had always been the popular girl, and Blake and I were the bomb couple. Now I was the butt of the joke.

I pulled away from Brenton and dashed to my car. I was so frustrated when I could not get the key to work. I just kept pushing the button and pushing the button and nothing would unlock.

"Sounds like you're relocking it," Brenton said.

Totally upset, I scolded him. "Why don't you leave me alone? I got this, okay?"

He took the key from me, pressed the button one time, and my doors unlocked. "Stay here with me and chill. You're not okay. Forget Blake. He doesn't understand what a great girl you are. His loss."

I grabbed my keys from Brenton, got in my car, and said, "Just leave me alone."

As I drove home, I realized I didn't have to be that rude to the one person all day who had been on my side. However, at that moment it took all my energy to calm down so I would get home safely. I made it a point to apologize later.

When I got home, my dad's car was not there. All the lights were off. I peeked into my parents' room. My mom was asleep. I got into my own bed and, after minutes of tossing, I drifted off too.

The next morning I woke up feeling really sluggish. It felt like I'd been hit by three linebackers and could not get off the field. However, I did pull myself out of bed. I had cheer practice to get to.

This was our last practice of camp. It was a Saturday. I had no pep in my step. I didn't care about warming up.

Coach Woods called out, "Captain Charli, you need to get them girls together. Let's go."

I followed her instruction. However, the team didn't follow my lead. After the third time of telling them to line up and not having them comply, Coach Woods took over.

Coach said, "Ladies, this is our last full day together. I expect you guys to give me more than what you're giving me now. How you practice is how you're going to perform. We've got football games coming up, and we have a big competition. The first one is major because how you rank determines whether you'll have a hard or easy road getting to the state competition."

Whitney vented, "We're exhausted, Coach. We've been at this for three weeks. Maybe you should blame our captain. She worked us too hard, and now look at her. She isn't even giving her all."

She was right. I had lost my zeal. Cheerleading was everything to me, and yet I was in a leadership role unable to get my team to focus.

"Charli, can I see you for a second?" Coach Woods said to me. "Play the dance over and over. Someone come up here and get it done."

"I'll gladly do it," Whitney said, flouncing her way to the front.

When I got into Ms. Woods office, I accidentally shut her door rather hard. She wasn't pleased at my melancholy demeanor. She crossed her arms and looked at me intensely.

"What is going on with you?"

I could not tell her my world was upside down. I could not say my heart had been stomped on. I could not tell her I didn't feel like going on. I just looked at her.

Coach said, "You made a commitment to this team and to these girls. They need you. I was behind you being captain because you have something special. I need you to dig way deep. I know we all get a little moody during that time of the month ..."

With that comment I checked out on her grilling me. Shoot, I knew how to deal with my menstrual cycle. What I didn't know how to deal with was getting people to act right. My girls were mad at me because I was tough on them. Blake broke up with me because I was busy. My dad was abandoning our family because he needed someone to "understand" him. I mean, really, in addition to being upset, I was angry.

All this happening to me at once made me feel like it was my fault. But I didn't deserve any of this. Like Coach said, I had a responsibility, but so did everyone else in this world. I just had to find a way to go on without my life being as

perfect as I was used to it being. I told Coach all she wanted to hear and jogged back out onto the floor, finished the rest of practice, and hoped my heart would stop hurting.

Leaving the gym, I felt depressed. I had lost my team. I had lost my friends. And I had lost my man. However, I certainly did not want the world to know about it. When I heard Eva going on and on about Blake's new adventures, I knew as soon as I stepped outside I was going to be hot for two reasons. Yeah, I knew ninety degrees was going to feel instantly miserable, but seeing Blake flirting with the world would tear me apart.

Eva said, "I don't know why she wouldn't just give it up to him. That boy is too fine to be dissatisfied. She better be glad she's still sort of my girl or I would ..."

"You wouldn't do nothing," Ella said to her. "Charli's getting on my nerves too, but we're not going to betray her."

"Tell that to Whitney. Look at her hands all over him," Hallie said, since she was in front and able to see in the parking lot.

She turned around to face Ella, Eva, and Randal. I was behind them, and Hallie felt like she'd said too much. My big-mouthed friend put her hand to her mouth.

"Oh my gosh, Charli! I didn't know you were right behind us," Hallie said, trying to explain.

The other three turned around. Randal had an I'm sorry look on her face. Ella mouthed the words "Sorry." Eva shrugged her shoulders like, *You get what you get*. Then without real concern, they all kept walking.

Sure enough, the sun beamed on me like I was in a hot oven. The real sweating occurred when I was most uncomfortable. There was no way I could prepare myself to see Blake leaning on his car with his hands on Whitney.

"You're cute, but you're in high school," she said, "and you're a junior too. My man's in college, honey. Take your hands off the thighs." She lifted both Blake's hands off of her and tossed them to the side.

A few other seniors ran up to him, not caring that he was just sixteen. My car was not that far away, but it seemed like miles. I knew Blake could spot me. I did not know whether

to look directly at him or to intentionally look away.

When I looked down, I heard a strong, forceful voice say, "Black, are you okay?"

I looked back and realized that it was Blake's dad, Coach Strong. I did not want to appear wounded, but I was keeled over. I wasn't hydrated, and I was hurting.

"Yes, sir, Coach. I'm good, sir," I said, lying to him and myself.

Coach Strong asked, "My knucklehead son giving you problems?"

Blake had to be looking over here because he stepped away from all the girls, went over to some of his teammates, and tried to act as if he was not showing off. I was in his dad's PE class in ninth grade, but since Blake and I started dating, he spoke to me sparingly.

I wanted to say, "Could you talk to your son? Could you tell him he's making a huge mistake? Can you make sure he knows I'm the only girl he needs to be with, and he's messing up his life? These girls just want to get with him, give it up, and give him something. Come on, Coach, help me out ..." But I knew it was not my place

to share Blake's business with his father. Blake had serious issues with his dad. Since my mom and I weren't close, I understood. Blake and his dad were surely night and day. It was dark or light, never sunset, and if there was any chance the two of us could get back together and work things out, I knew I needed to keep my mouth shut. Certainly I would not say anything to Blake's father to get him into trouble.

"You know, I got a younger daughter at home," Coach Strong said. "She's just going into the seventh grade, but I'm going to tell you like I tell Lola. No joker is worth losing yourself, and I know how you feel about my son. If he breaks your heart, if he doesn't act right, if he mistreats you, move on … always someone more deserving of you. Right, Brenton?"

And I jumped because I did not even realize his nephew was on his other side. I certainly needed to come out of my daze. I was desperately trying to keep it together.

"See y'all later," Coach Strong said, not waiting for either of us to say anything.

He yelled out to Blake, "Straight home, son! You got some chores to do."

"Yes, sir," Blake called out quickly.

"Come on, Brenton. Dang," Blake shouted across the parking lot at his cousin.

A part of me thought he did not want his cousin talking to me. Another part of me realized he was probably just taking out his frustration on his cousin because he was embarrassed about his dad calling him out.

Either way, Brenton jogged off. Then he turned back to look at me and said, "My uncle's right, you know. Always somebody better waiting ..."

He turned back around and was gone. I wanted to say, "Coach Strong said somebody more *deserving*, but if that's what you want to think—that you're better—that's fine." Then I saw Jackie head over to Blake with her girls. Blake was all standoffish until his dad pulled out of the parking lot. Then he pulled Jackie real close and kissed her hard. I do not ever think we kissed like that before. I realized that this breakup was going to be extremely hard.

I felt Brenton's heart trying to console me. Maybe someone else was waiting? Maybe someone else was better for me? Maybe I didn't deserve to be hurt so badly?

Blake saw me standing there. Why would he just disrespect me like that? He knew I still loved him. He looked my way and kissed her again. I couldn't get to my car fast enough. I could feel Hallie, Ella, Eva, and Randal's eyes on me. I looked up, and I was correct. But they offered no sympathy. They piled into Hallie's car and drove away.

When I saw Blake tell Brenton to get out of his car and find another ride home, and Jackie got in the car with him, I could not stop the tears from falling. I did not want anyone to see me broken, but the truth was I was more than broken. I was shattered.

I barely listened to any inspirational music on the radio. Usually I had to have the latest jamming numbers blasting, but as I drove home, I needed the uplifting songs to mend my spirit. However, when I replayed Blake's crazy actions in my mind and visually saw him all into everybody but me, I turned the radio off.

I was not used to seeing my dad's car in the driveway, but it was there. I was mad at him. He did not need to say anything to me. He did

not need to call my name. He did not need to try to act like everything was all right because I knew things were not good, and I was tired of pretending.

As soon as I entered the house, he had his arms wide open like I was supposed to go to him and hug him. Yeah, he gave me a car, provided for all my needs, and had an open wallet where I was concerned, but I needed loyalty and love. I did not need bribes. Maybe the reason why my mom and I bumped heads a little bit was because we were so much alike. She was not going to take being handled just any kind of way, and neither was I. So I walked straight on past him.

My dad said, "Wait, baby doll. Wassup with that? You can't give your dad a hug?"

Though he was a judge, he tried to act pretty cool. His problem was that he thought he was too cool. He thought could he get away with having another lady on the side. I was not buying it.

"Dad, just please," I said. I kept walking.

"What's going on, Charli? It's that Blake boy again. What did he do?" my dad asked, following behind me.

I went to the kitchen and wanted to make myself a sandwich, and he had the audacity to ask me to make him one too. I turned around and looked at him.

Then he snapped back, "I know you don't have an attitude. I just asked you to make a sandwich. Goodness gracious, girl. You are not paying any bills around here. What is the problem?"

"You're the problem, Dad!" I said, unable to hold it in.

Shocked, he said, "Excuse me?"

"Last night I was out and about, and I saw my father with some lady I did not know, holding each other all laughing, giggly, and stuff. It was crazy, and it wasn't right. You are the problem. What was that about, Dad? You're married, or did you forget?!"

He stepped over to me and raised his hand. I stepped back, and I guess he caught himself because he pulled back and didn't slap me. If he would have hit me, he would have been wrong because I didn't deserve to be punished for bringing out his indiscretions.

"What were you doing, following me? You're a kid, girl. You have no business being in mine! That was a colleague and—" he defended.

Cutting him of, I huffed, "Dad, are you serious? I just happened to stumble upon you and whoever she was in that black dress, and she wasn't going to a funeral, more like a night club. Your lips were practically touching hers! I wanted to follow you, trust me, I did, but I got lost. Another car jumped in front of me, so who knows which way you went? But when I got home at eleven, you were nowhere in sight. Colleague meetings run *that* late?"

"You misunderstood what you saw. You had absolutely no right to follow me. What were you doing out that late anyway? I'm going to have to talk to your mom about this. Did you talk to your mom about this?" he asked, realizing what he was saying.

I just went over to the sink and washed my hands. I put soap on them and was thankful for the wonderful aroma of the soap, which usually calmed me down. Unfortunately, the smell could not diminish the intense moment. I was getting more upset.

Quickly, I rinsed off the suds, dried my hands, and went over to the refrigerator. He was talking. He was saying all kinds of stuff. Who knew what he was saying because I refused to listen. Besides, the brash tone he was using was not right.

With lettuce in one hand and sandwich meat in the other, I turned to him and said, "Dad, I love you. I thought you loved Mom. I thought you loved us. But what I saw, what I know—though I might be a kid, I'm more mature than you think—wasn't right. No, I didn't tell Mom. I would never tell her that. I didn't want to break her heart, but you're breaking her heart anyway."

We both were startled when my mother came to the kitchen door and said, "Roger, our baby is growing up. I don't know whether to be angry that she saw what she saw or thankful."

My father didn't know whether to calm my mother down or come to me. Both of us thought that she was out doing her afternoon jog. My dad was so on a rampage, tearing me up for calling him out, that we did not even hear the door open. But there she stood with her world just as

shaken as mine—probably even more so because she was supposed to have a firmer foundation. She was married, for goodness' sake. They were going on twenty years. My dad was throwing all this away for nothing.

"How could you say that?" my father said to her.

With a vulnerable voice, my mom said, "Because she idolizes you. She puts you on a pedestal. You are the Honorable Judge Roger Black. The world admires you. You can do no wrong. But you *have* been doing wrong, and had I not seen it with my own eyes, I wouldn't have believed it either. And our daughter is right! You can't do this to us!"

"It wasn't what she thought—"

Needing to make this mess go away, I said, "Mom, I don't know if it really was what I saw."

"Don't try to explain it, Charli. Don't try to cover up for your father. I just can't believe that you didn't think you could come to me and talk about this."

"For what? So I could break up my family? You guys got to stay together. You guys got to work it out," I cried.

I now understood what had been tearing my parents apart. I so wished that I didn't know and had not spotted him. My dad's eyes welled-up. Thankfully, my dad chose to walk over to my mom.

She looked at him with an *It's over!* expression and said, "No more hiding. No more lying. No more trying to change your story. You've been caught, Your Honor. To think that you sit on one of the highest courts in our land—you have moral standards to uphold. What irony! You've been proven guilty, and the one person you love most now knows that you're not perfect. Wow, now you've been broken. Can you see how I feel? Losing something you really care about is hard. Well, deal with it, because payback hurts!"

CHAPTER 6

Sometimes Down

I hated running out on my father as he tried to comfort me. Though I loved him, I was upset with him. I certainly felt bad that my mom found out what I had stumbled upon.

I just wanted my pillow. As soon as I got in my room, I locked my door. I buried my head in it and let the tears flow.

School was about to start, and I would never have thought that I would be on the other end of fantastic. My world was upside down. Nothing in it was going right. The school mailed my schedule, which was all screwed up. I wanted to scream,

but what would that do? I had to ask myself a question: Did I bring all this bad karma on myself? Did I deserve to have everything snatched away? Was my tough situation my fault?

As if my mom knew what I needed, I heard a soft tap on my door, followed by the sweet words, "Baby, open up. It's Mom. Let me in. I want to talk."

As bad as I felt about all of this, I knew this had to be affecting her much worse. So I got up, wiped my face with the sheet, and headed over to the door. Her arms were extended, and I just fell into them like an Olympic swimmer dives into the water. And for a moment I felt so safe, so secure, so loved, and nothing else mattered except for the fact that I was her little girl. As much as I tried to be tough, sassy, grown, smart-mouthed, and independent, it was clear I needed my mother's protection.

Looking up from her bosom, I said, "I'm sorry, Mom. I didn't mean for you to hear any of that. I didn't wanna break your heart."

"Charli, I'm sorry you had to see what you saw. I'm sorry that this house hasn't been the haven it has been for you in the past. Life happens,

and it pulls people apart sometimes. This is hard on us both, and I don't want you to own any of this. Your dad's got to make this right. This is not your fault, and I don't want you to be bummed out about it."

"Mom, how can I not let this affect me? So much is going wrong."

"Yeah, but you must be tough, baby."

"Mom, Blake broke up with me."

Rubbing my hair, she said, "I'm sorry, honey. I know you really cared about him."

Continuing, I said, "And the cheerleading squad … they don't even want me to be captain anymore. Unlike your situation with Dad, I did some things that probably led to both of those situations going awry for me."

She lifted my chin to face her. "Well, honey, I don't want you to think I'm blameless in this whole thing with your dad."

"Yeah, but you didn't make him go out and cheat on you."

She looked away. She swallowed hard. My mom held back her tears.

"I'm sorry, Mom. I guess I shouldn't have said it that way."

"I know you're growing up, Charli, and some of these things I want to keep from you. But if I want you to be ready for the real world, we must really be able to talk. And that's probably your dad's biggest problem with me. It's hard for us to be transparent with each other."

"What do you mean?" I said.

Huffing, she voiced, "I don't make it easy for him to always shoot straight, bring me all his problems, all his issues, and all the tough dilemmas. I have him feeling like he's weighing me down ... like I want him to leave work at work and not bring it home. However, I've been doing some evaluating of my life, and I realize that he should be able to say whatever he wants. I've gotten so caught up in a lot of my civic organizations: PTA, the sorority, the church group, and everything else, that I am available to everybody but you and your father. I am not blameless in all this. I've got some things I must work on. Sometimes we go to our lowest point so that we can do self reflection. You're going into your junior year of high school, Charli. You've got a lot of great things going on."

"*Had* a lot of great things, Mom," I said to her, feeling melancholy.

"Well, getting a new car, being captain of the cheerleading squad, having a stud boyfriend, not having to worry about what a lot of kids have to worry about, like where you're next meal is coming from, paying the bills, having a roof over your head, being safe. None of this is your concern. You're a great student and you're beautiful. I figured one of these days that you were going to get a big head, and while I hate that you are hurting, being arrogant, cocky, and selfish is surely no way to be."

My mom had not been walking daily with me for the last couple of months, but she was right on with all that she was saying. Though I thought I was confident, I was alienating people. Though I wanted to stay focused on cheerleading, I had completely left out someone who needed me. Though I wanted a car badly, I got in the middle of what my parents wanted for me. I had gotten a little too big for my britches, and I knew it.

"So how do I fix all of this? I mean, I can't fix you and Dad. Blake's moved on with another

girl. Honestly, seeing him today hugged up on some other girl makes me think …"

"Okay, okay, okay, enough about Blake. Yes, let him move on. The right boy will come along when it's time. I told you that before. What about the cheerleading squad? If you feel like you lost their support, maybe you do need to step aside for a minute. But you're not a quitter, and you do have some assets that you can bring to that team. You're a smart girl. School's about to start. Let's go shopping so we can enjoy each other. The rest of the drama is going to work itself out. Though it is a little dark for the black women … I see light on the horizon."

I just hugged her. She left, and I turned on my computer, waited for it to boot up, went to my e-mail, and clicked on my address book. I pulled up all of the cheerleaders' e-mail addresses as well as Coach Woods's. I typed:

Dear Ladies,

First of all, I want to apologize for being overzealous as your captain. There's no excuse for how I treated you guys, and I do want the best for our team. Like I always truly believed,

I know we can win state; therefore, to help us do that, I am resigning as captain—effective immediately. Again, thank you all for your support, and I know the next leader won't make the same mistakes I did. Forgive me.

Charli Black

As I pushed send, I could only hope this e-mail would be received the right way. I knew I lost friends, lost respect, and lost my job as captain, but I did want to earn back their trust. This was the best way I knew how to do that. It was hard, but it was right.

It was the first day of school, and I felt like all eyes were on me at Lockwood High. You might as well call me the cowardly lion, as I couldn't face all the folks talking about me. Even though I could barely hear some of them, I knew what they were saying.

One girl rolled her eyes at me and said, "She thought she was all that. Now she has nothing."

This other chick laughed and said, "Blake's girl no more. He dropped her."

The dude that had much sweet style whispered, "The best cheerleader, but they certainly didn't want her to be the captain. Didn't you hear they fired her?"

The last comment he made was not true. However, they did not care that they heard the story wrong. And what did it matter anyway? I certainly felt worthless.

What was worse than feeling like a loser was being excluded from my girls. Walking into the school together had always been our thing. However, this year I had to watch them stroll in as a foursome. Looking fly, as I knew they would. Holding their heads up high, which they should. And working it like only they could. I realized how much I loved them: Hallie for her outgoing personality. Ella for her sweet heart. Eva for her bold sassiness. And Randal for her reserved demeanor.

They saw me, and I *so* wanted them to stop. I wanted them to ask me how I was doing. Maybe even tell me that I looked good. Would it take much of their energy for them to talk to me for a second and catch me up on their world? But they kept going, and it took every ounce of dignity I

could muster up to not run and hide. This was going to be a tough year.

My mom was with me to make sure I got my odd and even classes changed: AP English, Chemistry, US History, and Math III. I was so happy I had Musical Theater and PE, but I didn't want too easy of a schedule. I still wanted to impress college recruiters. Therefore, I had French III and Statistics. College here I come. My focus would be on making sure I was ready for the next level. SATs were coming up in a couple of months. My GPA was a 3.5, but I needed to crank it up because the schools I was interested in required a 3.75. I had work to do, and with no social life, I could do it.

Finally, I made it to lunch. Even the unpopular kids heard I was branded a chump. Their table was not full, but I got the mean eye not to sit there. Other tables I passed were full. The table all the way back in the corner had a couple of science geeks and a couple of empty chairs. When I asked them if I could sit there, none of them even looked up. I wanted to plead and beg for my friends to take me in, but this was going to have to do.

When I reached to pull the chair out, strong hands pulled it out for me. "Can I sit with you?"

I looked up and smiled for the first time that day. Kind Brenton Strong was standing with a tray, and he was sporting his brand-new, first-day-of-school digs rather well. I motioned for him to sit down.

"You know, word's out I got the plague. You don't wanna catch the 'unpopular' disease. You might wanna sit somewhere else," I warned him.

"I think you know me well enough by now to know that I don't care what people think or say. You shouldn't either. Not looking as good as you do, anyway," Brenton said, stepping up his game.

I knew he liked me. I was not dumb. He had been flirting for the last couple of months. But to pull out my chair, give me a compliment any girl would blush over, and stare me down … what was up? What was his angle? With all I was dealing with, I did not even have time to figure it out, so I just started eating. Brenton kept staring.

"*What?*" I said.

"Is something wrong?" he asked, taking a bite of his sandwich.

Lots of giggling filled the air. I looked over and felt like I had been kicked in the gut again. Blake walked into the cafeteria; my depression went up a notch.

"That can't have you hung up," he said, as he motioned his head in the direction of Blake.

Seething, I said, "He's a trip. Isn't he supposed to be going out with Jackie? What's up with the short skirt he's talking to now? So tacky."

"Yeah, you still talking like you care. Want me to go get him for you?" Brenton said with a little attitude, clearly upset that I still had feelings for Blake.

I didn't tell him not to get Blake, and I didn't tell him to get him either. Then he put down his food, turned my chair toward his, and said, "Why don't you get it? He's moved on. You're gorgeous. You're smart. And you deserve more."

"Yeah, whatever, says the boy who has no girlfriend," I uttered.

"It's not like I can't get one but whatever," he said, even more frustrated with me than I was with Blake.

As he was about to get up, I placed my hand on his wrist. "I'm sorry. I was completely out of line. I didn't mean that at all."

Brenton was coming at me hard. I simply wanted to come back at him harder, but he was coming at me because he cared. I needed to show him I appreciated that.

Trying to get Brenton to understand, I said, "It's my fault with Blake ... that's all. It's hard for me to get over him ... knowing I'm the reason he's gone."

"Are you kidding?" he said. "He's my cousin, but he had a wandering eye way before you didn't answer some call. He should've appreciated that he had a girl with a life. He's not the only one who can have it going on. The thing I really dig about you ... yeah, you're fine. You're fly. You're fearless. All that's cool, and I mean ... no brother wants to have an ugly girl ... I'm just saying."

I smiled.

"No, seriously, what I admire ... what I like ... what I really dig about you is that you always got something going on. If it's not

you studying or thinking about the next level, you're trying to take your team all the way to the state cheer deal, or you're going to volunteer somewhere. You're always on the move, and Blake was a little jealous of you, frankly. You need a man who's confident enough in his own game ... that can be proud enough of his girl doing her own thing too."

"And what? You wanna be that guy?"

Getting closer, he whispered, "You know I do."

I was really uncomfortable because I felt lost ... because that always upbeat girl that he was talking about was gone. I did not know her anymore. So I looked down, embarrassed, but he took his masculine hand and placed it under my chin and pulled my face upward toward him.

In a smoother tone than Brenton had ever used, he said, "You have no reason to walk around here feeling down. Get the Charli Black we both know back. And if you can't find her, let me bring her out."

Then he leaned over and kissed me. It was like the cafeteria stood still and so did my heart. Brenton Strong had it going on.

"Okay, just because it's the first day of school and it's a long day, don't come into cheerleading practice acting like y'all can't give it your all," Whitney said, picking up right where I left off.

I was stretching when Coach came over to me and said, "I'd like to talk to you about your e-mail."

Whitney yelled out, "There's nothing to talk about. We all got it. Resignation accepted."

Coach sternly replied, "Whitney, lead the cheer, please."

Whitney cheered, "Everybody do this … and this … and this … everybody do this. Our first game is Friday. Let's turn it up, girls."

I scratched my head. Gosh, Whitney was annoying. If I was *anything* like that, I wouldn't be able to handle it either. When Coach Woods and I got to her office, she said, "So uh, what was the e-mail all about?"

I really wanted to say, "Duh. What part of it didn't you understand? Like, I spelled it all out on the computer. Did you comprehend the fact that I was such a witch that I needed to quit?" But all of that would've been jerk language. So not wanting to be disrespectful, I smiled.

"Yeah, I understood what it said," she said, picking up my body language. "I don't know why you said it. Yeah, you were difficult, but you were difficult for the right reasons. You want us to win; you don't wanna boss people around just because. You have high standards. Maybe you were a little brash in your tactics, but sometimes some of these girls need to be pushed. You're an excellent cheerleader, and you wanted to make sure everyone else exuded excellence. We need you. Look at the alternative, and I love Whitney to death. She's a scholar, but she's a snob. Everybody knows you had a hottie, and you were dissing him for this team. From what I hear, his ego got bruised, and he couldn't take it. He couldn't stand that he was second. He was second to cheerleading. Your commitment, your dedication, your accountability to this team was phenomenal."

Still not feeling good about my tough actions, I said, "I'm just not the right person, Coach."

"To lead anybody you must have that 'it factor' ... that support from them ... that willingness to follow your lead."

"I had that when they elected me, and I got the big head somewhere along the way. I don't

know. I was humbled quickly. I messed up."

"Which means you learned from it. Don't walk away from all of that."

"Yeah, don't walk away, because if Whitney stays up there and continues to be the lead, I might have to yank some of her poor weave out and then quit," Eva said, surprising me. Coach gave her that *Watch your mouth!* glare. "Sorry, Coach."

I was shocked to see her standing there. She wasn't alone. Ella, Hallie, and Randal were with her.

Coach smiled, walked to her door, and said, "Y'all talk some sense into this girl."

Dropping my head, I said, "Why do y'all care?"

Rubbing my shoulder, Ella said, "Your e-mail said it all."

"See ... we took this test," Hallie blurted out.

"Huh?" I was real confused, and Randal was tugging on her to hush.

Hallie continued, "It will just take a sec. I'm going tell her. There is a test in the book, *The Five Love Languages of Friendship*, and we found out that you're a task person. You can't help but to

be on people about doing things because that's just who you are."

"I'm confused," I said, knowing I was at a disadvantage for not reading the book with them.

"Like Hallie said, it's this book called, *The Five Love Languages of Friendship*. It has one test for marriages, one for jobs, one for the kids, and then there's one for friendship," Randal said. "It basically says that you have to understand how people show their love, and you can't love on them in your love language, but you gotta love on them in theirs. And they have five basic languages that we all fall into."

"We probably have all five in us. When you find out what your predominate love language is, your friends need to know so they can show you love in the way you need it, not in the way they want to give it. You can't push the way you feel loved onto others and expect them to respond," Eva said. "But you also have to know theirs so you don't become selfish. If you know how they need love, then you can give them just what they need. For example, my love language is treasure."

"Yeah, we know that," Hallie said. "We can't just come to your birthday party and bring just any old thing. It's gotta be thought out."

"Yeah, that's right. Y'all know it and it's coming up," Ella said. "And mine is touch." She kept rubbing my shoulder.

"Mine is talk," Hallie said. "You gotta tell me I'm doing okay. You gotta tell me you care. You know I wanna hear it. So when you say I'm doing bad, it really, really affects me."

Randal said, "And mine is time. Just all five of us being together means so much to me. And, Charli, you were task."

"Okay, I'm task. What does that have to do with you guys coming in here saying I need to stay captain? I am still confused. I was horrible, and I deserve for you all to never ever be my friends again," I confessed honestly.

"You're right. You do deserve that," Eva said, keeping it real. "But I think it was you who said we all need grace from time to time. It just wasn't the same first day of school without our girl with us."

Ella took my hand and said, "You know the word is out that somebody got a cool kiss today."

Randal chimed in and said, "Because we were not with you, we missed it. It just wasn't right."

"And because you're task," Hallie said. "We learned it's a part of your nature for things to get done. You wanted us to be on time, and you wanted us to know the cheers. You wanted us to do all the moves right because you love us. You care, and you went a little overboard, but you didn't want us to sink. Whitney is being a brat. She wants power and control. We know now that was not your issue. We feel like if we stay on you and make sure you stay in line then we can help you be balanced."

"Yeah," Randal said, "but still be a task manager and get things done. There's nothing wrong with time management."

"You guys forgive me?" I sniffed.

"Do you forgive us?" Eva stepped over to me and asked. "I told them we needed to just drop you. Instead of getting so mad, all we should've done was come and talk to you until you listened, not cut you off like that. That was wrong. That's not what best friends do. That's not what we do to each other. The five of us are more than

friends. We are sisters. We gotta make sure that's never broken."

"So you captain or what?" one of the senior cheerleaders said from the door.

"If you guys want me," I said, still overwhelmed by their gestures.

"Well, Whitney's out there running her mouth, and I'm speaking for the all seniors out there. We want you."

I didn't deserve a second chance, but the fact that I was getting it made me all mushy inside, like mashed potatoes. Getting a group hug from the girls, I knew I wouldn't change anything. Yeah, I was out of control, but I really learned to appreciate others. When I was on the outs, I learned so much about me and how to treat people. Now, things were looking up. My mom and I were bonding. My girls were back in my corner. I had gotten an unexpected kiss that felt great. And because of what I went through, I had learned to be a better me. It wasn't totally bad that I was sometimes down.

CHAPTER 7

Forever Cool

No, Charli's not going to be the captain again!" Whitney screamed when she found out the squad's decision to not accept my resignation.

I did not know Whitney that well, but I did know being captain meant a lot to her. It was hard being in that seat. Though some of her tactics were annoying, I could use her help. And instead of alienating her for good, I needed to figure a way to get her on my team.

Seeing Whitney's disappointment and wanting to fix it, I said, "Coach Woods, I nominate Whitney Alexander as co-captain."

Eva was standing right next to me. Guess she felt if Whitney wanted to brawl, she had my

back. At least she was with me until I made that statement. Then Eva hit me in my gut. Others grunted and made derogatory remarks.

However, I stood firm, meaning what I said, even though I knew it was not what Whitney wanted—she did want to be captain over us all, after all. This was some consolation. She may not be the first one in charge, but she'd have some power if she joined me. Shoot, last time I heard, something was better than nothing any day. Her eyes started sparkling. The frown she had on her face turned to a smile.

She came over and stood beside me and said, "Really? Are you serious about this recommendation?"

"Yes, I mean if you are okay with working with me. I know your pep and professionalism can take us a long way. Whitney, let me be clear. All I want to do is win. There are twenty of us on this squad. Why can't two of us lead it?" I asked. "If you are willing, we can be stronger."

Whitney's attitude softened. She realized I was not blowing smoke to cloudy up the air and confuse her. I was being true.

"Girls, how do y'all feel about this?" Coach Woods stepped in and officiated.

"Well, as long as Charli's captain and Whitney is co-captain, I'm fine with it," Eva said, giving me the eye.

Hunter, the sophomore, said, "If Charli says this is what she wants, we should support her. She does have our best interests at heart. Next to Charli, Whitney is the second best."

Whitney said, "Thanks, Hunter. I think."

Coach Woods looked at Whitney. Whitney nodded, accepting the position of second in charge. We voted and practice was over. Before I could get out of the door with my girls, happy to head out and just hang out with them for a minute, Whitney stopped me at the door.

Somewhat emotional, she said, "Charli, thanks. Nobody's ever stepped up for me until today, and it meant a lot. I want you to know working with you will be a joy. Here's my cell number."

She and I talked for a few minutes. It was neat that she admitted she was brash too. We agreed to keep each other in check. My lesson there was, if you find out what people who give

you grief are needing, and help them fix their issue, your life can be fixed too.

At the restaurant later, I had a big smile plastered on my face. My sisters, and that sounds so good to say, wanted to pay for me. The pancakes from IHOP never tasted so good. The company was not bad either. Seeing the four of them laugh at stuff—because I had been out of the loop for a minute, some of the humor went over my head—just made me sit back and appreciate the fact that I was so glad we still had each other. I was thankful that what we felt for each other was able to bring us back together. I was really blessed that our love was true.

"Did you guys see Leo from gym last year?" Ella said, as she cut into her french toast.

"Yeah, we've got English together," Hallie said, like it was not that big of a deal.

Ella said, "He's huge!"

"A lot of the football players are," I said, thinking about Blake. "Coach Strong has them on a strict regimen so they can pass the eyeball test."

"The what?" Randal asked. She frowned like the concept sounded ridiculous.

I was no expert, so I said, "I'm just remembering stuff Blake said. The eyeball test is when scouts from the colleges come over and look at players. They are looking for a certain athletic build. If you don't have the right height, weight, and physique, then you might be a good player but you're not D1 college material. A lot of the guys at our school are trying to go to the SEC and ACC."

"The *what*?" Ella asked, making me know my girls needed a football lesson.

"The top southern conferences: the Southeastern Conference and the Atlantic Coast Conference," I said. I threw my hands in the air, expressing that they needed to diversify their knowledge of the game.

"You were around Blake way too long," Eva said to me. "We just cheer for a touchdown. All that other stuff is extra."

"Yeah, and really overrated," Randal said, finishing up her food.

"I think I'm ready for a boyfriend," Hallie said out of nowhere. "I have no idea where I'll find one."

"Well, take your time," I told her, reflecting on my drama with men.

"Yeah, who wants a boyfriend?" Eva said, smirking. She had one up on the boys. "They want to be players, but they don't like it when girls like to have fun. I'm not going to let one tie me down. It's our junior year; I'm going to enjoy it."

"Yeah, but you don't want the wrong name for yourself," Randal said, referring to Eva being a little too loose.

With much attitude, Eva said, "You just get some business, then come back and talk to me."

Not taking it personally, Randal threw her hands up. Eva winked at her. Ella hugged Randal to make sure she was cool. I smiled at them all.

It was fun to see the five of us stating our opinions. We were all big headed, strong willed, and direct, but we knew how far to push each other and not to get on each other's nerves. I told them how much they meant to me. It was a serious moment of tenderness.

When I got home, I saw my dad moving things out of the house and putting them into his car. I rushed over to him and threw my arms around him.

"Dad, you can't go. We can work this out. Please stay."

My mom came over and said, "You're dad's going to leave for a while."

My dad cupped my face and said, "Yeah, but your mom and I are committed to working on this thing. Just need a little time apart. Don't worry, pumpkin."

As my father drove away, my heart sank. Though they had to do things their way, my soul did not feel good at all. I could only hope my dad would truly come back.

It felt really good walking into school with my friends. What a difference a day made! I was no longer on the outs. I was with my girls. I was a part of the in crowd, but I saw those who were not popular standing alone, looking disappointed and upset when people frowned at their outfits, hairstyles, or kicks. Instinctively, I went out of my way, speaking to every loner I saw.

Well, until Brenton came up to me and said, "Okay, you've passed me a couple times. I guess I need to stand by myself for you to notice me?"

Letting him know he had swag, I said, "Well, you were with your boys and everything, so I didn't want to step in the middle of all that."

"I guess my kiss wasn't that good because today I can't even get a hello, much less an instant replay. Unless you want to prove me wrong," he said, as he stepped in a little closer.

"No affection in the hallway!" Eva said, as she pushed me on to class. "Call her if you want to catch up with her. She's got an iPhone. Text her."

As me and my girl dashed to class so the bell would not catch us, I smiled. Brenton was truly into me. He noticed I was trying to make others feel good.

Walking with Eva, I was lost in thought when she said, "Yes, he likes you, girl."

We had an even and odd schedule, which meant we had four classes on odd days and four different classes on even days. This was an even day, and Eva and I had PE together. The bell rang right before we stepped into the gymnasium. Thankfully our teacher, Coach Woods, gave us grace and motioned for us to hurry and get ready.

When we went into the locker room to change, I stopped walking because I saw Jackie

talking to a few of her girlfriends. They were looking at pictures on her phone. High-fives were being dished out like she'd won the lottery, gotten an engagement ring, or won the lofty Pulitzer Prize. Had Blake asked her to be his girl?

"I can't go in there," I uttered. But I was with Eva, and of all my friends, she was the last one that was going to let me punk out.

"Hey, y'all! Excuse us. You're standing right in front of our lockers."

"There's no names on any of these," said Dajezah, who was really large and sassy.

Eva stepped to her and said, "Just because dance girls don't have lockers, be informed that varsity cheerleaders do. Move, big mouth. They're right here. That's why they're locked up."

Dajezah shook one of the locks to irk Eva. The other girls laughed. There was no movement.

Eva stood firmer, wanting Dajezah to do something stupid. "Move now!"

"Ugh, you can just ask us nicely," Jackie said. "You don't have to be rude or anything. Just because I got your girl's man doesn't mean you have to be salty."

More upset than I could explain, I tried to calm myself down before I spoke truthfully. "I'm standing right here, Jackie, and I'm clearly aware of everything that's gone on. You don't have to rub it in my face."

As much as I wanted to say Jackie was ugly, I couldn't. I definitely could see why Blake found her attractive. So did a lot of other boys, the way she flaunted what she had. Not hatin', I had to admit that her body was tight, and she was not a dummy either.

Showing she wasn't a true jerk, Jackie said, "For what it's worth, Charli, I am sorry."

"You're sorry for what," I vented, realizing this girl had truly broken the *Leave someone else's man alone!* rule, and she did not deserve my forgiveness. "Disrespecting the fact that I had a boyfriend? Come on, Jackie. Are you really sorry? You did everything in your power to take Blake away from me. You're sorry for what? That you pranced around practically naked right in front of him so he wouldn't have to imagine what was underneath your clothes. You wanted him to see. What are you sorry for? I mean really … you knew he had me, but that didn't matter to you.

But now that you're his girl, do you understand how vulnerable you are to have a guy like him be *your* guy?"

"Yep, because these girls around here don't respect no relationships," Eva sneered. "I admit, I'm a player like the boys, but I don't go after taken merchandise."

"Please, when you're all used up, nobody wants you," Dajezah said, as a couple of her girls gave her dap.

But I pulled Eva back, because the ghetto in her was rising up. Jackie looked away. She knew she had done me wrong. Truthfully, it certainly was not totally her fault. It took two to tango, and Blake was dancing with her. When we stepped out of the locker room that was obvious.

Before stepping onto the gym floor, Eva said, "Brace yourself."

I took a very long, deep breath, "Blake's in this class, isn't he?"

"Yeah, and ... um ... Jackie just ran to him. He's cuddled up with her," Eva grabbed my hand to keep me strong, reminding me of how Ella always used touch to show love.

When I looked over at Blake and Jackie, they were laughing and smiling. Honestly, it was hard to see Blake happy with someone else. His two boys, Leo and Landon, strolled over to us. Leo was the one Ella had said had gone from a stick to a stud. Landon was a tall, lean cutie pie too.

"Boy, are you on steroids?" Eva quickly said to a beefed-up Leo.

"I told him, right?" Landon teased, irritating Leo even more.

Leo sarcastically uttered, "Ha-ha-ha. Just 'cause some of us don't get in the gym, no need to hate on the results."

Landon put up his muscle to impress. Unfortunately, the result was not a cut look. We all laughed, including Landon, as his arm clearly wasn't as dynamic as Leo's. Leo smiled, feeling redeemed by the coarse joking. Then Landon was looking Eva up and down.

"What you looking at?" she quickly said to him.

She was into older guys. She had always only dated upperclassmen. Now that we were juniors, seniors were the only ones who had her eye. I could tell Landon's feelings were hurt.

"I didn't even come over here to talk to you," Landon said to her, trying not to be embarrassed. "Charli, we just wanted to let you know that you're still our girl. We still cool, right? We know our boy lost his mind, got another girl and all, but we like kicking it with you guys."

Leo added, "Yeah, Brenton, Blake, Landon, and me, we hadn't hung out with y'all in a while. We don't want all that to be over. But you understand why Blake needed you so bad."

Getting revved up like a race car engine to go hard, I said, "I understand, Leo. He thought I wasn't there for him. What was so important that he needed to talk to me about? I do not know but …"

"You ain't know?" Leo asked me.

Landon looked at Eva. "You didn't tell her?"

Eva looked away. Landon covered his mouth like, *Oh snap! No wonder you never got back to him.* Leo threw his hands up, motioning for one of them to tell me.

I blurted out, "Tell me what?"

Eva whispered, "Blake's mom has cancer."

Those words hit my core. "Mrs. Strong, really? Oh my gosh."

"He found out around the time he kept calling you. He was freaking out. His dad was going crazy. We tried to be the rock for him, but I wasn't tryna hold a brotha's hand. But Jackie was there," Landon explained.

So much became clear. If he would have just said that his mom was sick, I certainly would have made time for him. I wonder if he thought that I would just instinctively know what was going on and connect with his pain? I was not a mind reader though. I knew Blake wouldn't just go after the next pretty face. But I had let him down to his core. It didn't matter that he was laughing with Jackie right now. It didn't matter that the coach was trying to get us all to huddle up for the lesson. It didn't matter whether Blake would completely go off on me. I had to let him know how I felt. Right. This. Second.

So I rushed over to Blake and said, "Jackie, could I talk to Blake?"

At first she wasn't moving. I gave her a look that said it all: *I respect your territory*. She nodded and stepped away.

"I just wanted to say I didn't know about your mom. I'm so sorry. I hope she's okay."

"She's got a battle ahead of her with testing, chemo, a possible operation, and other stuff, so it's hard. But it means a lot that you care," he said, finally looking at me the way he used to.

"Of course I do, and I owe you an apology for not being there." There was an awkward silence for a moment. Finally I said, "I wish we could go back and fix it all, but it is what it is. I just want you to know that my feelings can't completely dissolve. I do want us to be friends if that's okay with you and the new girl. I won't do her like she did me."

Blake didn't know what to say. He just looked, stared, and nodded. I walked away from him, knowing that he was not going to be mine, but happy we were not going to be enemies. Sometimes that just had to be enough.

It was Friday night lights and the first game of the season: So many of us had been looking forward to this after a long, steamy summer. The Lockwood Lions were taking on a big 5A school from Warren Robins, Georgia. The press said the road to the Georgia Dome, where the football state championship was held, started here. The

team who won would have the best opportunity of winning it all in December, but this was late August and the heat was on.

All the cheerleaders looked good. Our uniforms were sparkling. Our bows were perfectly positioned atop everyone's head. Our pom-poms and megaphones were lined up straight. All the folks passing by smiled and gawked. We had it going on. Even Whitney understood her role and was not trying to take over. We had practiced so many sideline cheers and made up new ones that I knew would not bore the crowd.

All should have been well, but it was not. Blake was on the fence, touching Jackie's hair. She was flaunting a skimpy little outfit. And he was looking. I was having a hard time with it.

We started cheering close to kickoff time. However, I threw my pom-poms down because I had no pep. I started to walk briskly toward the gym, but my girls came along side me.

"What's going on? We saw you looking at him, so there's no need to front like Blake doesn't have you all twisted up," Eva said, as if she'd just figured out the hardest SAT question. "He's not all that."

"Yeah," Randal said awkwardly. Her sister-girl strength didn't come naturally to her because she felt uncomfortable with her mixed heritage. "Child please, let Jackie have him. It's going to get old before you know it, and he'll be coming back your way."

Needing them all to head back to their positions, I said, "I just can't cheer tonight, okay? Her screaming Blake's name ... He was supposed to only want me. How am I supposed to deal with this? How am I supposed to get out there? How am I supposed to act like everything is all right? I just can't do it, okay? You guys are great. Whitney's calmer. You'll have a better night without me putting a damper on it. I am not in a cheerleading mood right now. You don't want me to completely ruin this great moment."

Ella surprised me when she said, "Look, I know I always say the sweet stuff, but forget his behind. You don't cheer for Blake. You cheer for Lockwood High School. You are the captain because you lead us. We can't cheer without you."

Randal put her arm around me and said, "I know I always tell you to be modest and to take it easy, but in this case forget that advice.

Besides, there's another guy who likes you. Forget Blake."

And Eva said, "I know I'm always brash, but I understand you care about him. This hurts you, so I won't say move on. But seriously, Charli, it is *his* loss."

"And I know I'm always loud ..." Hallie said before she leaned in and whispered in my ear. "You have it going on. You live for cheering. I would kill to have your skills. Do not let anyone steal your joy."

A tear was rising up in me, about to ruin my perfect makeup. My girls had moved me. They cared and they made sense. I had to find a way to move on. If I was real with myself, he really wasn't everything I deserved, whether his mom had cancer or not.

"What do *you* want?" I heard Eva say, as I looked up and saw Blake pitifully standing there. He wanted solace; I was the one who needed comfort.

"Can I talk to your girl for a second?" he asked Eva's permission.

Something weird happened at that moment. Though Blake was standing right in front of me,

I saw Brenton in the background. I could not explain the connection, but while I thought my heart wanted the one directly in front of me, it actually was beating pretty rapidly for the one a few feet behind. Blake turned and saw what was holding my attention.

He said, "I just wanted to make sure you were all right, but it looks someone else can make sure you are."

I looked in the stands and saw Jackie starring nervously. Something in the way Blake was looking at me made me think I could say, "Can we have one more chance? Can we give it another go? Can I be your girl again?" And he probably would have gone for it.

He asked, "So you going to pick up your pom-poms again? I saw you throw them down."

"Oh, so you're watching me?"

"Don't tease me, Charli. I know I lost a good thing in you, and I understand now that my cousin cares for you in a way that I'm just not ready to."

"Thanks for admitting that."

"Well, you're special."

Though Blake cared, I knew he wasn't what I wanted. He wasn't what I needed. Brenton was right. I did have goals, dreams, and aspirations. I would not mind male company, but I was not trying to lose myself to please a guy.

"We are going to be friends, right?" I said to him, remembering our gym class talk.

"Yeah, if my cousin will allow that," Blake teased, peering back at his boy.

Seeing the pregame clock tick down, I said, "Go get them tonight. Blake, be careful. I think Jackie wants a lot from you." I could feel her ears all the way over here in our conversation, wishing she knew exactly what we were saying and making assumptions.

"I'm going to go in now. We got to win this game. My dad catches me out here talking to all these girls, you know I'ma be in trouble."

Before he got to leading the true business of the night, I asked, "How's your mom?"

"Just keep praying."

"You know I will."

He touched my face and jogged off.

Brenton was jogging past me, and I said, "Wait, hold up. Can I say something?"

"What, you want to tell me you're back with Blake?" he asked in an aggravated tone.

"No, that's not who I'm with. That's not who I want." I touched Brenton's shoulder pad.

"Oh, so you know what you want now? I saw you pitch a little fit earlier."

I huffed. Shoot, did everyone see me storm off? I had to keep my emotions in check from now on. Cheerleaders were front and center, and they had a rep to protect, an image to uphold, and a team to cheer to victory.

"Yeah, but I realized that's done, and if you're serious about all that stuff you have been saying to me, maybe we can give it a go."

Coach Strong yelled from the field house, "Brenton, boy! Get it in here!"

But before he left me, he pulled me into his arms. Then slowly and softly, his lips touched mine. Watching his fine, caring tail run off, I realized I was down no more.

My girls came all around me. They squealed. After they settled down from being happy about my romantic interlude, I told them how much they meant to me. With all hearts and minds clear, we ran to our positions.

It was time to go to work. I was a leader. I learned not to take that for granted. And though the night wasn't how I imagined it a couple months ago, it actually was perfect. Even when going through the drama, I had to stay savvy and remember that the down times would end. When times get tough, don't stress. You can make it if you stay forever cool.

STEPHANIE PERRY MOORE is the author of many YA inspirational fiction titles, including the *Payton Skky* series, the *Laurel Shadrach* series, the *Perry Skky Jr.* series, the *Yasmin Peace* series, the *Faith Thomas Novelzine* series, the *Carmen Browne* series, the *Morgan Love* series, and the *Beta Gamma Pi* series. Mrs. Moore speaks with young people across the country, encouraging them to achieve every attainable dream. She currently lives in the greater Atlanta area with her husband, Derrick, and their three children. Visit her website at www.stephanieperrymoore.com.

WANT A DIFFERENT
point of view?

JUST *flip* THE BOOK!